I0629408

HEATHER MANNING

Tossed Together

PUBLISHING

Copyright © 2019 by Heather Manning

All rights reserved. No part of this publication may be reproduced, stored or transmitted in any form or by any means, electronic, mechanical, photocopying, recording, scanning, or otherwise without written permission from the publisher. It is illegal to copy this book, post it to a website, or distribute it by any other means without permission.

This novel is entirely a work of fiction. The names, characters and incidents portrayed in it are the work of the author's imagination. Any resemblance to actual persons, living or dead, events or localities is entirely coincidental.

Second edition

This book was professionally typeset on Reedsy.
Find out more at reedsy.com

Tossed Together is dedicated to my supporters. Thank you to my family for tirelessly reading blurbs I write.
I wrote the entirety of this book while attending college. I met a whole new network of friends and professors who will not hesitate to tell anyone we meet that I'm an author. Thanks for your shameless promotion.
Thank you to my readers. I would not be here without you.
Finally, all glory be to God, who gave me these made-up worlds in my head, and the ability to put them down on paper.

Foreword

Hello and thank you for joining me on this journey. *Tossed Together* was originally published while I was in college. Since then my publisher has closed, and I decided it was time for my *Ladies of the Carribean* series to be out and accessible for those who wanted to read it. Thank you for your support, and I can't wait to share many books to come with you. Please keep in touch with me via my website, www.heathermanningofficia l.com or my social medias.

Chapter 1

P ort Royal, Jamaica
1696

"Well, well, well. What 'ave we got 'ere?"

Lady Aimee Dawson skidded to a stop to avoid smacking into the burly man who had stomped out in front of her. A glance backward told her she had lost Captain Matthew Emery a while ago. Which was good. Well, she did not want to lose him for good—he was her ticket back home, after all—but she did not want to see him any time soon. They had gotten into yet another fuming argument, and she just needed some moments away from him.

"What's a pretty lady like ya doin' runnin' around the streets o' this wicked town all on her own?" The burly man took a step forward. His bushy eyebrows made his scarred face almost animalistic. Aimee stepped backward, out of his reach, but bumped into another body. She shrieked and whipped around so fast her hair slapped her in the face. Another man, this one

1

much taller and thinner, stepped closer, trapping her between the two men. Their combined foul body odor made her bite her cheek in disgust.

Aimee's hands fisted at her sides. "If you gentlemen will excuse me, I need to be somewhere right now, and you are in my way." If they kept her here much longer, the stupid preacher-turned-sailing-captain, Emery, might catch up to her, and she did not feel capable of dealing with that ninny right now. The sight of several pistols strapped to each man's chest and a twinge of fear halted her heart's beating. These were dangerous men. Maybe Captain Emery didn't look so bad after all.

"Little lady, 'ow 'bout ya come inside with us, and we will help ya find where ya need t' be." The shorter, stout man grabbed her wrist and drew her close. His breath reeked of rotten fish.

Aimee tried to shake off his grip, but he held tight. "Let go of me!"

The tall man grabbed her by the waist, his greedy hands gripping her closer. His foul stench hit her nose. Why, he probably had not washed in months! If the first man had not had a tight grip on her arm, she would have reached into her sleeve and breathed through her handkerchief. Oh, what she would not give for her sweet, lavender-scented handkerchief right now.

"C'mon, little lady. Let's take you inside," the taller man said as they shoved her toward one of the two-story buildings lining the street.

What were they going to do with her? Nothing Aimee cared to stick around to find out. She kicked at the men's shins. They chuckled. The stout man released his grip on her arm, bent down, and hefted her over his shoulder.

Aimee thrust her legs forward. Her boot knocked the tall man in the head. He yelped and bent down to his knees, cradling his neck in his hands. Aimee tried to launch herself to offset the other man's balance, but to no avail. He swung open the door to the building in front of them and roughly tossed her inside. She hurtled onto the floor in a heap of pink petticoats and ribbons.

"You're a feisty little thing, aren't ya?" The taller man entered from somewhere behind them, rubbing the back of his head.

Aimee righted herself and took in her surroundings. She was in…a tavern, or possibly…a house of ill repute. Definitely not a place a lady like her should be seen in. Everyone stared when she entered, but they were soon back about their business. Men sat around several large tables, downing whiskey or rum or whatever it is people like them imbibed. Some were asleep. Some were shouting at each other and eyeing up their weapons, no doubt preparing for a fight. Others entertained scantily clad women perched in their laps, brushing kisses against their necks. Aimee shifted her gaze. No decent women acted like that in public.

And the stench. Oh, the stench. Yet again, Aimee yearned for the sweet solace of her perfumed handkerchief. She spun around and tried to make her way out the doorway, but both men blocked it with their bodies.

Aimee felt like stomping her foot in frustration. However, that was not what ladies did, and she was a lady. Or at least she was trying to be. When she was around people like Captain Emery, she seemed to regress to the days of her childhood. Apparently these rude men brought that out in her, too. "What do you plan on doing with me here?"

"You're just gonna stay with us, and we'll help ya have a good time, missy."

Aimee threw her hands on her hips. "I do not want to have a good time and certainly not with the likes of you!" She could feel her face heat as she shouted, fear fueling her anger. It probably was not ladylike, but she was more of a lady than any of the other females in the room, so she supposed she was allowed to digress some. "I *demand* you let me go *this instant!* I…you don't even know who I am! Granted, I don't know exactly what you are planning for me, but I am one of the most eligible young women in all of London. I have dozens of wealthy gentlemen and nobles vying for my hand at home, and my father and brothers are some of the most influential men in England. And if anything happens to me, I promise every one of them will come down here and this little establishment will be shut down and you all will be locked in prison!" She shoved her pointed finger at the tall man's chest.

Both men had the audacity to throw their heads back and roar with laughter. Aimee's face burned in embarrassment and anger. How dare they?

"Come on, little lady. We'll get you comfortable while we discuss exactly what t' do wit' you."

Seeing their tall figures close in around her, Aimee's mind fled back to a time years ago, when she was just a little girl. She had been playing outside at church with the other children after a service. A new boy had just joined the congregation. He was unlike the rest of them: he had no nursemaid, no mother or father. His clothes were threadbare and dirty. And he was crying. Alone, inside a circle of other children who were laughing at him. Just as she was now, alone in a circle of taunting men.

On that crisp fall day, Aimee had walked inside the circle of children and held the boy's hand, urging her friends to leave him alone. He had looked at her with tear-stained eyes and almost seemed afraid. And then her father walked by and pulled her away, scolding her, a lady, for getting in the middle of such a fuss.

What would her father think of her now?

* * *

His lungs burned. Captain Matthew Emery let out a groan of frustration. Why, if he weren't out in public, he would slam his forehead against the nearest wall. Repeatedly.

What was he to do with this blasted woman? Of course, he did not *exactly* care what became of her, he supposed, but she *had* been placed under his care, under his trust. "God, why are you doing this to me? Why did you leave her with me?" Matthew forgot there was a sea of strangers around him until a few sent puzzled and some not-so-kind glances his way at his exclamation.

He let out another sigh of frustration. It was her problem now. If she wanted to get into a fight with him over what plans they had that evening and then run away because she did not like the way he spoke to her, that was for her to deal with. Not him. She was more so his passenger than his responsibility. So if she got murdered or worse on these barbaric streets, that was not his fault. Was it?

Blast. Of course it would be his fault. This woman would

be the death of him. He could not wait to get back to England and be rid of her. Except she attended his church. He would dread each and every Sunday morning.

Matthew sped up. Where could the little brat have gotten to? Surely not far. "Lady Dawson? Aimee?"

Some men standing nearby in his path chuckled. "Lost your girl, didja?"

Matthew ignored their gibes and shoved past them. Lady Dawson was most certainly not *his girl*, and she never would be. "Lady Dawson! I know you are upset with me, but running away makes no sense. You are just going to get lost, or injured, or…" His words trailed off as he came upon a horde of men swarming around the entrance to one particular establishment. Upon further glance, Matthew realized it was a house of ill repute. He cringed and glanced away. Nothing good came out of those houses. He knew that from experience.

What on earth could have gotten so many men to gather around that building at once? A certain phrase, however, caused him to pause.

"How much'll ye give me for this wench? She claims t' be a real, English-bred lady!"

"I assure you that you will regret this for the rest of your—"
Smack.

A feminine voice cried out in pain. A familiar, feminine voice. The voice of a real, English-bred lady that Matthew happened to know.

Men cheered.

No, it could not possibly be.

Matthew shoved his way through in an attempt to view what they were all gawking at. He nearly keeled over when he took in the sight. Lady Aimee Dawson stood atop a raised platform inside the tavern, wrists tied together. Two burly men, one short and one tall, flanked her on either side. Her pink gown was torn at the already low neckline, exposing much of her chest. Matthew coughed and forced himself to look away, but his gaze moved back to her yet again. Her eyes, cold and hard, were red as if she were about to cry or had already shed some tears. The right side of her face was darkened by a…bruise, perhaps? Was that already blooming from the smack he had heard when he walked up?

"Hey, let us see what we're gonna buy!" An ill-kempt man shouted from the crowd.

Matthew felt his throat tighten in anger. He knew what was going on, and no matter what had passed between Lady Dawson and himself, he did not wish this fate on her or anyone. Why had the fool woman decided to run from him anyway? If she hadn't pitched a fit, she would not be in this ugly predicament. *God, please help us. What am I supposed to do with her?*

The taller man at Lady Dawson's side leaned down and raised her skirt up past her knee. Matthew couldn't help but notice the woman's slim, shapely leg as she struggled against the men around her. He had never seen a woman's practically bare leg before. Blinking multiple times failed to remove the image from his mind.

Lady Dawson jerked away from the men, releasing the taller one's grasp. But the short man kept his grip and tugged her skirt up even higher.

Matthew had to do something. But what would make these men stop? He could have this entire mob of men upset with him, and that would not solve his problems.

A grizzled-looking man in the front ran a hand up Lady

Dawson's calf, yelling something that sent a chill racing down Matthew's spine.

"Stop!" Matthew shoved forward through the crowd, but his presence seemed to have no effect. "By all that is right, stop this nonsense!" A heavyset pirate bumped into him, nearly making him tumble to the ground. He used the momentum to surge forward to the front of the crowd at the center of the tavern.

"Leave the lady alone!"

Silence dominated the room, so unusual compared to the men's constant yelling it made his ears ring.

"An' who might ye be?" The taller man stepped forward, and placed a hand on Lady Dawson's shoulder.

"I…I am…"

Lady Dawson's eyes flashed with more fire when she recognized Matthew.

"I am…"

"Well, speak up, then! Who do ya think ye are?"

"I'm Lady Dawson's…fiancé. And I demand you release her at once!"

Nausea bubbled in Matthew's stomach at the statement. It would kill him if he actually was this spoiled woman's fiancé, but what else could he say to make them leave her alone?

"Yer her fiancé, huh?" The tall man stopped in his tracks, eyeing Matthew as the room rumbled with laughter that rolled into full-out guffaws.

Heat singed Matthew's ears.

"An' the lady? What does she have to say about this?" The burly man stomped over to Lady Dawson and leisurely ran a hand down the length of her arm before leaving it to rest at her waist.

Lady Dawson recoiled from the man's groping touch, yet he followed her and allowed his hand to linger even lower on her waist. Matthew's blood boiled to the point where he wondered if his head would explode. No one should be touched like that against their will. The tall man grabbed a fistful of her golden curls and yanked her closer to him. "What is yer relation to this pup?"

The lady bit her lip until her teeth drew a drop of blood. Her emerald eyes darted about the room before glaring his way. Something Matthew had never detected from her lined her face: resignation. Panic surged through his body as he realized the full depth of this situation. Either he lied before all of these people and God, or he would have to witness this woman being sold into a nightmare. Although he hated the idea of lying, and he by no means felt kindly toward Lady Dawson, he could not allow her to face the torture that awaited her.

"Aye...the man is my betrothed." The words creaked out of her throat, one raw from tension and fear.

* * *

Aimee resisted the urge to squeeze her eyes shut. The bread and cheese she had eaten earlier in the day threatened to rise from her stomach and spill onto her slippers.

"Oh, now? Ye're a betrothed woman, huh?"

Aimee hesitated as she eyed the man. If pretending to be engaged to Captain Emery would earn her freedom, she would certainly agree to it. It was just a small falsehood. "Aye. I am promised to him." She was surprised at the amount of calmness she managed to exude.

Her stomach rebelled, but she managed not to embarrass herself. What would she do if she truly was engaged to Captain Emery, the one man she despised most in this world? The very thought was a nightmare to her. But if it was true, then she would be freed from this terrifying fate. This terrifying fate that became closer and closer to becoming a reality with each moment that passed.

Engaged to Captain Emery? What a preposterous idea. And yet, still, it was less preposterous than what was about to become of her. Hmm. The choice was difficult, and yet the answer was clear.

"Aye, I am his fiancé. This is true. I have been engaged to him, and he is an important part of society back home in London. If something happens to me here, he will ensure that you and all of those involved will pay. Deeply. You will regret the day you allowed this to happen to me."

Please, God, please tell me that this is all just a dream. Please let me wake up. Just moments ago, I was running through the streets, upset over some petty argument with Captain Emery. Now I am to be his bride, or be abused by these men? No. It cannot be. Let me wake. Please let me wake.

"How much will you give me then?" exclaimed the taller man. "How much will you give me since you claim she is your betrothed? She must be worth a pretty penny to you."

"Well…" Captain Emery choked and his face reddened as he attempted to speak. "She is worth everything. No amount of money is too great for her." His face reddened as he spoke the words that were most certainly a complete and utter lie.

Aimee respected him much more in that moment than she

had the entire time she had known him. Since when had he ever done anything good to her, much less attempt to save her life? If not her life, then at least her dignity.

"Please, Captain—Matthew." Aimee's voice was reduced to a croak. "Please help me." She'd never been this humiliated before.

Aimee lunged forward, but her captors held her in place. "No, you aren't going anywhere. Not today."

"No!" Captain Emery shouted from the crowd. He leaped toward her and tried to free her of the vile man's grip. But he failed. They pulled her backward, up to the front of the room once more. A lone tear escaped its lashed barrier and trailed down her check. So this was what would become of her. What would her mother and father think back home? What of her older brothers? Would they care? Would they come to her rescue as she had told the others?

Probably not. Everyone thought she was simply the spoiled brat that she always acted like. She leaned forward, attempting to free her hand to wipe away the tear that trailed down her cheek. *Oh, what am I to do? What am I to do?*

Would her brothers come to save her? Surely they would miss her when she was gone. Her big brothers meant the world to her, and a life without ever seeing them again made her heart ache. Well, that would have to be all right. Because she would never get out of here. Not alive, at least.

Dear God, I am sorry for all of the wrongs I have done you. I am sorry about how selfish I was. I wish I had never been so terrible to Captain Emery. I wish I had been kinder to my brothers. Even when I was younger, I was selfish. I am sorry for the time I ripped that doll out of the girl's hand at church. I could have given it to her, and my father would have bought me a new doll the next day.

I probably would have gotten an even better one. The newest doll in all of London. I have always been terribly selfish, just as Captain Emery always accused me of being.

"The woman is my fiancé, and I demand you release her. It's that simple."

* * *

Matthew wished with every bone in his body that he was carrying the pistol his sailors always encouraged him to tote around town. But the blasted weapon was so heavy, and he had no intentions of getting into quarrels with dangerous men, so it felt pointless.

Well, now he would give anything for the ability to protect himself and Lady Dawson.

One of the men ran a hand across the lady's curves, a menacing smirk across his grotesque face. Fury dashed through Matthew. No man had a right to touch any woman like that, even a spoiled minx like Lady Dawson. His fists clenched at his sides.

"I'll let her go. On one condition." The man ran a grimy finger down the length of her cheek.

"Anything," Matthew breathed. As long as he could get her out of here, return her safe to her family, and forget this nightmare.

"Ye marry the wench here an' now."

Matthew could swear he heard the woman whimper.

"M-marry her? Now?"

Silence met his question.

"Well, there's no one here to perform the ceremony," Matthew said.

The short man leaned back his head and released a cackle. "Ye're sittin' in a room full o' cap'ns, mister. They're legally allowed to marry folks. I don't believe ya. Prove it to me. Besides, I've never been invited to a weddin' before."

Lady Dawson whimpered once more.

"How 'bout we all marry her and get t' share 'er," a pirate on the crowd exclaimed.

Lady Dawson's face flushed bright red. "Oh God, help me."

Matthew studied her expression. Her eyes were dark and wet with mortification. Although this entire situation was her own fault, pity welled up in his heart. She had stayed admirably strong during this time. No matter how conniving most women were, no woman deserved the fate of a prostitute. Matthew sucked in a deep breath. He allowed the oxygen to fill his lungs, no matter how polluted it was with the stench of the tavern. "You will let me leave with the…my….fiancé, if I marry her here and now? You will leave her unscathed?"

Lady Dawson's eyes brightened.

Dead silence hit the room.

"Aye. I may own this tavern, but I am a decent man. I respect t' union of marriage. If you are truly promised to her and she agrees to it, it must be true. Who wants to marry these fine young people?"

Grumbles stained the air.

"Who would wanna marry 'em if that means losin' a chance at the lady?"

Another man leered and said, "Do we get to make sure they consummate the marriage?"

"Silence!" The taller man's voice rang across the room, at once silencing the horde of men. "Now, this is my establishment, and I found the lady. Therefore we do everything on *my* command. An' if ye have a problem with that, feel free to leave my tavern!" He turned to his shorter compatriot. "The lady won't do it. She does not seem like the type that wants to marry a stranger. Now. Who among ye has the right to marry a couple?"

"I will. I served as a captain for a year," a young man, voice laced with a Spanish accent, said.

"Very well then. Come on now."

The man stepped forward. Matthew felt the blood drain from his face. This was truly happening.

A glance at Lady Dawson told Matthew the feelings they experienced were mutual. Her normally rosy cheeks were now the color of fragile porcelain. Her rosebud lips had become sheet-white. They were in for some serious trouble.

Chapter 2

Aimee exited the tavern twenty minutes later, arm in arm with her *husband.*

Her *husband!*

"Blast!" she muttered under her breath, but immediately covered her mouth with a hand when Captain Emery cast her a harsh look.

She had never quite envisioned her wedding day playing out as it had. For heaven's sake, she had never allowed the thought of marrying the man next to her cross her mind! She could only hope he would agree to forget about this farce the second they escaped the town. Suddenly, Emery stopped and tugged on her hand, deep into her hair, fretting with her hairpins.

"What?"

He nodded to the side. Aimee had to stop herself from gasping in shock. The men poured out of the tavern like rats, spewing obscenities that brought heat to her cheeks.

"They say they want me to kiss the bride."

Panic laced his eyes, while bile rose in Aimee's throat.

"Kiss me then," she said.

His face scrunched up as he leaned forward and braced his hands on her shoulders. The man's features were grim and stiff. He lowered his mouth to hers.

Aimee had kissed many suitors in her life. She had never kissed a man she hated. A man who was her husband.

After a quick brush of his lips, he pulled back. It almost looked like he was going to be sick. Aimee bristled. He may hate her, but that was no reason for him to feel sick after a single kiss. Was she that undesirable?

The men around them roared in displeasure. "That's all ya got!"

Emery groaned, snagged Aimee by the waist, and drew her tight against himself. She barely had a chance to catch her breath before he slammed his lips onto hers and didn't relent for what seemed like hours. He tugged her closer still, deepening the kiss.

The crowd erupted into a tangled mess of catcalls and whistles, cheers and angry shouts. Only after all of the ruckus had died down did Emery pull away. After offering a wink—which looked unnatural on his stoic face—to the hungry crowd, he tucked her arm against his elbow and walked away at a breakneck pace.

Aimee nearly fell over herself trying to keep pace with the man, but after a few blocks, they had escaped the rough-and-tumble crowd.

She fanned her burning face in an attempt to cool down. "*What* was that, Emery?" Heaviness weighed on her chest, making her feel as if she didn't have the strength to even stand on her own.

He paused a moment, studied her, and then jerked her forward with a tug of the arm. "We have no time to waste."

The heel of her shoe caught on a dip in the cobblestone pathway and snapped in two. "Oh, blast!" The words escaped her mouth before she caught them. Emery attempted to continue their romp through the city, but how was she to continue with a broken slipper? Yet again, bile rose in her throat at the thought of her recent marriage. She was going to be sick, as well.

She tugged on his arm, causing him to jerk to a halt.

"What is it?" He rolled his eyes.

"My heel. It broke."

"That's nice, but we need to *hurry back*."

"I can't!" Aimee shaped her face into her most alluring pout and folded her arms across her chest. She wanted to get away from the filthy group of pirates and no-goods just as much as he did, but her feet would be ruined with blisters if she hobbled back like this to the boarding house.

* * *

"We must hurry, unless you wish for all those men from the tavern to know where we are staying." Matthew leveled a cool stare at the woman.

She continued to pout, puffing out her red lips and crossing her arms over her rounded chest. But her womanly wiles did not work with Matthew. He was not stupid.

"Come on. Or I will leave you to fend for yourself with those men at the tavern."

"But I cannot possibly walk like this!" She huffed, hurtling herself forward a step and falling against his chest in over-exaggeration.

This woman could cause even the most mild-mannered man to tear his hair out. With a groan, he heaved the nuisance of a woman up in his arms and continued on his way to the boarding house where they were staying while his ship was being careened.

She kicked frantically, but Matthew tightened his grip. "I am not hurting you, I'm helping you." When she moved like that, her curves pressed against him pleasantly. He quickly cleared his mind of that thought. He *despised* this selfish woman, and that was that.

"Get your hands off of me, you bumbling oaf!" She shoved his chest with her palms.

"No, we need to hurry. Just stop struggling."

"I'm…I'm…" The lady moaned. Something warm slid down his chest, seeping through the open neck of his shirt. Matthew gasped in horror. The woman had cast up her accounts on him! He gagged uncontrollably.

Lady Dawson—he supposed he should call her Aimee, now, since she was his wife—wiped her mouth with the back of her hand. "*Now* will you let me down?"

"Gladly." He abruptly released his grip on the woman, feeling only a little remorse when she dropped to the ground on her bottom in a puff of pink petticoats and lace. Really, she deserved the sudden fall.

Aimee huffed and stood, before she stopped to examine the stain that dripped across his shirt and onto his trousers. "I…I apologize, Captain." She cupped her hand over her mouth.

"Excuse me." The woman doubled over and once again emptied the contents of her stomach, this time onto the ground and not on him.

Matthew couldn't help but notice that she had managed not to get any vomit on herself or her pretty, pink dress. No, her first bout had all landed squarely on *his* chest. Fighting his gag reflex, he dragged a handkerchief out of his waistband and tried to wipe up the mess.

"Blasted woman," he muttered under his breath. Aimee Dawson—Aimee Emery—would be the death of him.

* * *

Aimee could not conceal her anger. It was not as if she had purposely done that. She had simply become sick from the terror she felt when the realization of her past and current situation had sunk in.

"I did not mean to do that, Emery."

"Certainly, woman. Certainly." He stepped forward, and with one swoop, tugged his shirt off over his head. Aimee's breath stuck in her throat at the sight of his bare chest, and she averted her gaze.

Several passersby stared at him for a moment, but Aimee supposed the sight was not that unusual due to their location near the docks. Workmen were often stripped of their shirts when they were loading cargo onto the ships.

Emery gingerly folded his shirt and continued on the way back to the boarding house.

"Wait!" Aimee lunged forward, but her broken heel snagged her step and she nearly fell once more.

The man sent the barest of glances over his shoulder and continued on.

"My slipper is broken, remember?"

"I remember it well, milady. Take them both off and walk barefoot if it is such a hindrance. We are almost back."

Aimee was tempted—really, really tempted—to pluck off her shoe, and *throw* it at his retreating back! Unfortunately, she chose to behave like a civil woman and removed her shoes before running to catch up with her boor of a husband. By the time she made it back to the boarding house, she was certain her stockings would be torn beyond repair.

Biting her cheek to refrain from crying out when she stepped on a stone, Aimee forged on. What a mess she had gotten herself into. Just a few short months ago, she had been living happily in London, attending parties and wearing the finest clothes. Then, her best friend, Eden, had run away from home to escape marriage to a boorish man named Lord Rutger.

Aimee shivered at the memory of the day she had learned of her friend's escape. Pressing her fingers together, she still remembered the determination that had driven her. As any best friend would do, Aimee had grabbed another friend, Ivy, and demanded they set off together in search of Eden to make sure she was safe.

With a sniff, Aimee managed to hold back the tears filling her eyes. If only Ivy was here now. She was the most logical of the trio of friends and had persuaded Matthew, the owner of a merchant ship, to sail them all to the Caribbean in the hopes of finding Eden. Aimee bit back a groan. Out of all of the merchants in England, she doubted a more disagreeable one could be found. She had dreaded the thought of going on an endeavor with a man that she disliked so, but, as Aimee's bare feet scraped over the filthy ground, she still knew she would make the same choices if given the chance.

The worry which consumed her at Eden's disappearance had overcome her so she had to leave home, telling only her closest brother, Sebastien, that she was going and he needn't tell her father. Sebastien had agreed to make up a cover story for her disappearance, about how she decided to visit a friend in the country for a good long while.

Another pebble ground into the sole of Aimee's foot, and she struggled not to whimper at the pain that grew with every step. Everything had gone smoothly, up until they arrived in the Caribbean and discovered Eden was actually quite well. By the hand of God, the ship Eden had stolen passage on was captained by a kind pirate who had soon fallen in love with her. Eden was happily married when Aimee and Ivy had gotten to her.

The sights and scents of the rough town around Aimee now overwhelmed her and she struggled to breathe. With Eden set on staying in the Caribbean, Ivy and Aimee needed to return home, but their ship had needed repairs. Aimee's chest ached with sorrow and understanding as she recalled the day Ivy set off with another ship in order to get to her baby brother in haste. Which left Aimee alone with Captain Emery. Aimee glared at his retreating back before despair weighed her limbs and encumbered her steps. And now, look at her. Married to the man.

Could life get any worse?

* * *

An hour had passed since they had reached the boarding house, and Aimee's sentiments remained the same, the spark of resilience within her had become an inferno, seeking any opportunity for escape. No matter how her feet ached and her soul cringed, she would not surrender this battle easily.

"I consider this to be a marriage in name only, Aimee," Emery said from across the room.

Aimee released a growl that had been forming in her throat for some time. "Goodness, I expected that much, at least!" The fool.

The man had changed into new clothes and washed up immediately after returning to their boardinghouse, and he now paced in circles across her room. Fairly soon, he would rub a hole in the already damaged carpet. "Good." He glared at her in disdain.

"I hope you know I expect to get an annulment as soon as we reach London," Aimee said.

"No, I will not get an—"

Aimee tugged on a strand of her hair. "We could pretend it never happened. You and I are the only ones who know about this…unfortunate circumstance. However, I suppose word could spread to your crew, but we could ask them not to speak about it and—"

"Aimee, I am not going to agree to that. As much as I may regret my actions, I made a vow to you before God. There is no way you can persuade me to break that vow. I am a man of my word." His fists clenched and unclenched at his sides.

Chapter 2

"You expect me to *stay* married to you? Are you daft?" Aimee's voice jumped an octave. "What about *money*? How on earth can you provide for me? Why, I had plans to marry a rich earl or a lord—goodness, a *prince*, even! Not...not a *sailor* like you! Oh, what will my father think?"

"I may not be a prince, Aimee, but money is not everything. Earthly possessions mean nothing. I have enough funds to support a wife, although I never planned to marry."

"Never planned to marry? Then why can we not just pretend this never happened?" Aimee's head grew light. Could she really be tied to this man for life?

"Because, as I said, *princess*, I made a vow. That may mean nothing to you, but it means much to me. Now give it a rest, I beg you." The man ran a hand through his golden-toned hair. If only he were not so cruel, he would be quite handsome.

"All right. I will stop discussing it. For now. But when we get to London, my father will never let this continue. He has plans for me to marry someone important. Someone influential." Aimee threw herself down on the ragged chaise lounge that lined one wall of her boarding room.

"You know, princess, for someone so appalled with the prospect of being my wife, you should consider what marriage would be like to one of your wealthy earls or lords." He slammed a fist against his hip.

Aimee grabbed the fan from her pocket and fluttered it in front of her face. "What do you mean by that?"

"You feel like I am such a horrible person to be chained to, but have you considered the personality of the wealthy men you dream of? You could very well be just as unhappy with them as you are with me. Money does not equal happiness."

"No, I will not." Aimee snatched a small looking glass from

the nearby table and checked herself as she fussed with her hair. "I will be comfortably wealthy and have a handsome husband at my side. I will wear the latest fashions and eat fine food. What more could I ask for?"

Emery had the gall to chuckle. "Some would say love."

Aimee always felt the need to defy this man. "And what would you say?"

"Respect. Faith. Kindness. All of these are important in a union."

"Most of which you do not have."

"How dare you say such a thing? You do not even know me, princess."

"Oh, I know enough about you. I know how you have treated me the last few months on your ship. Goodness, I know how you have treated me since I can remember meeting you! You act as if I am a…a criminal. I know you could never hold respect for me even if you were forced to do so, and I have never seen any kindness from you."

* * *

Matthew knew he did not like the woman. Not one whit. But had he always been so cruel to her that she would have such a dark opinion of him? *Well, the blasted woman deserves to be treated as I have treated her.*

Matthew shook his head. Aimee was a fellow child of God, and he supposed he should get around to treating her like one. Besides, she was his wife now. Treating her like she was the devil incarnate was not a promising way to begin their marriage.

"Aimee, I would like to apologize for the way I have treated you in the past."

The woman threw back her head and laughed. "Chivalrous attempt, but I will not fall subject to your pitiful charms. Please leave. We are getting nowhere with this conversation."

Matthew allowed a sigh to slowly escape. "Very well. I will see you tomorrow, *princess*. Sleep well tonight. Try your best to not get yourself into trouble."

The woman shook her head and waved him away. Matthew gladly left her room and shut the door firmly behind him. What an infuriating woman. And to think, he would be chained to her for the rest of his life!

After Matthew found his way to his room across the hall, he sank down on the nearest chair and rested his forehead on his hands. "Dear Lord in Heaven, what have I done?" He scrubbed his hands across his face. "Married her. *Married her.* I married the one woman I despise most in the world!"

His mind swam with all the thoughts of what lay ahead of him. He might as well give up his dreams of becoming a preacher. What kind of a preacher would have such a self-centered, self-righteous bride? That would set a horrible example for his parishioners. *What have I done?*

Matthew needed to get his mind off of such thoughts. What was there to do, though? He heaved a sigh as he pulled out his Bible. The sacred tome was well-worn, its binding frayed, many of its pages torn. It had been with Matthew through everything since he was eight years old and Reverend Dobbs had gifted it to him. This book had seen him through every kind of struggle imaginable, so surely it would help him now.

But Matthew found he could not bring himself to open the beloved book today. It was that blasted woman. He was afraid if he spent much time with God's Word this evening, he would see how stupid he had been. How could he have let himself marry that prissy, bossy little thing? In his eyes, if he would ever marry, he should marry for love. He should marry someone he wished to protect and cherish and care for. Not someone who repulsed him, who made his life miserable. He had half a mind to barge right into her room and tell her that he had no interest in being her husband, that he could not fulfill the vows he had promised her before God. But there was no way he would allow himself to do that. He would not stoop to that level. He had already lied once today, and he did not plan to break a vow, too.

And yet, Matthew had seen moments of kindness in the woman. She had always been one to stand up for the down-trodden. Back in London, she had encouraged the ladies of the church to start a charity for orphans. Just a few days ago, she had come across a lost kitten near their boardinghouse and she had offered the scared little thing some food and affection, until its mother came along and they were assured it was in good health. Aimee did have a soft spot in her, but she had rarely shown it to him.

Their kiss flashed in his mind for a split second. She was the first woman he had kissed, and he was loath to admit that the action had been shockingly pleasant. He had tried his hardest to hide that fact from Aimee after it had occurred. Obviously, he must never allow something like that to happen again.

Something else; put your mind on something else, you fool. Matthew forced himself to think through what he had been doing earlier today, when he had been a bachelor—before he got into an argument with his soon-to-be wife and chased her across town.

Ah, yes. He was going to hire a translator. Typically, wherever Matthew went, he stopped to help spread faith to more souls throughout the edges of the world. In some of the Caribbean colonies, it seemed as if men of the cloth were difficult to find, so many villages were happy to welcome a preacher to bring a bit of civilization to town for a few weeks. He tried to move between the islands as often as he could. This time, Reverend Dobbs, his good friend from England who had taken him in as a son and was once a missionary, had informed Matthew of a need for pastoral care in Haiti. Although many of the natives had died off on that island as it was being colonized, an amount survived who had no ties to Christianity, and Matthew felt something inside tugging to go back there. One of the chiefs he had met on a previous trip spoke some English, but Matthew could not hold all interactions through him. However, in order to reach the native people, he needed to find a translator.

Matthew rubbed his thumbs against his temples in an attempt to fight off the headache forming behind his eyes. Well, finding a translator could wait. He needed rest so he could forget about his vicious little wife and begin to think clearly.

Chapter 3

Aimee glared at her ogre of a husband over the cup of tea she sipped at their morning meal in the boardinghouse. She pinched her cheeks in an effort to wake herself up further, for she was afraid that any minute now she might fall over asleep, using her dry, crusty slice of bread as a pillow. On second thought, maybe that crust of bread would serve as a better pillow than the pitiful pillow the boardinghouse offered. A shudder escaped her body, causing her to tremble. She had not gotten a good night's rest. Emery raised a judgmental eyebrow at her before he bowed his head once more and commenced silently reading from his Bible.

At the table, no less! An unladylike growl of frustration slipped past her lips. He was certainly untrained when it came to table manners.

Emery closed the book, careful to keep his finger on the page he had been studying. "Is there an issue you wish to discuss, oh fair princess?"

Oh, she could match him at false sweetness. After all, she came from London's finest society. It was not natural to be honest in that kind of environment. Aimee pasted on her sweetest, most flirtatious smile. "Yes, indeed there is, kind sir."

"And, pray tell, what might that be?" He spread his arms wide, piercing her with his glare.

"You are being positively obnoxious! Who taught you your manners? One does not read at the breakfast table." Aimee fought the urge to scream indignantly, but she knew that when she gave in to such childish fits of passion, the man held even less respect for her. She wanted to do her best to survive living with this pig of a man.

"Well, what does one do instead at the table with someone like you?" Emery leaned forward, no doubt deliberately bracing his elbows on the table to mock her.

"A normal gentleman would with me engage in conversation, but obviously that task is far above your intelligence level." Aimee rolled her eyes.

He ignored her second comment. "All right. Did you sleep well, princess?"

Aimee gingerly set her chipped teacup down on its mismatching saucer. Really, this ramshackle boardinghouse was much below her station. "No, I did not sleep well, Emery. It would seem as if the prospect of my unwanted marriage as well as the horrible bed in this awful place do not agree with me." A yawn escaped her lips, and she made no effort to politely camouflage it.

The infuriating man's lips upturned in a rude grin as he stretched his arms behind him and leaned his head back on his folded hands. "Ah, perhaps the mattress was not soft enough for the princess, so she could not sleep? Poor thing."

Aimee resisted the urge to scream at his demeaning tone. A few deep breaths calmed her down before she was ready to speak. "Emery, I would be forever grateful if you would refrain from speaking of me in that fashion. Since I am your…your w-wife, now, I think that you should treat me with respect."

"As my wife, you vowed to submit to me. But I do not foresee that happening any time soon."

Before she realized what she was doing, Aimee was already on her feet and three steps closer to her *husband*. She wanted to slap him, to wipe that horrible smirk off of his cocky face. But she should not. She closed her eyes and counted to ten. No, maybe twenty would calm her more efficiently. Or thirty.

"I am going to retire to my room, Emery. Perhaps I will be able to get some sleep. Let me know when we are going to leave this wretched town, and I will be ready." Aimee spun on her heel and exited the room before she could do something stupid.

Like punching her husband square across the jaw.

Rather than punching her husband, Aimee decided she would pen a letter to her father back in London and beg for his help. If her brother Sebastien had kept his word and made an excuse to her father about her disappearance, this situation would come as a shock to him. However, she decided it was time he knew that she was stranded in the Caribbean with a boor of a husband and not having a leisurely visit to the country. Between her father and her four brothers, someone was bound to think of something to get her out of this mess of a marriage. Aimee searched the room for paper and pen. She was honestly surprised when she found some. Apparently, she had underestimated this low-level boarding house.

Frantically, Aimee addressed a letter to her father, detailing what had happened and where she might be found with Matthew. She ran it downstairs to the clerk at the front desk and asked him to send it off for her.

She walked back to her room, feeling no more relieved. It would take her family a long time to find her if she was a moving target.

God, please help me.

* * *

God, please help me.

Matthew swallowed a groan as he studied the man before him. Eric Honeysett, he believed the name was. And while this applicant seemed the absolute perfect contender for the translator that Matthew needed for his mission work—he was fluent in French, as the natives were—something about him set Matthew on edge. Maybe it was the licentious way Mr. Honeysett had interacted with the barmaid. It made his skin crawl. However, this man happened to be the only person Matthew knew of who was in need of a job and qualified for the position. The other applicants he had spoken to only knew a few words of French.

Mr. Honeysett brushed a lock of shiny black hair behind his ear. "As you can see, sir, I am perfectly suited to work as your translator."

Perhaps part of what set Matthew on edge was the man's narcissism. Nonetheless, Matthew had no choice but to accept him. He needed a translator. "Well, Mr. Honeysett, consider yourself my employee. You can meet me at my ship, the *Cross's Victory*, first thing tomorrow morning. Do not be late." He reached out a hand and was disappointed in his new recruit's limp handshake.

"Thank you very much, sir. You will not be disappointed."

* * *

Aimee battled to contain her golden-blond curls in the elaborate coiffure she had pinned them into earlier this morning as a gusty, hot breeze threatened to tear her hours of hard work apart. It was this blasted ship. She despised it.

After a day, Emery had ordered her back on his stupid ship to prepare for their journey. No, not their journey home, but their journey to another island to suffer in the miserable Caribbean heat. A church mission, he had said. She stifled a laugh at that concept. While she supported the idea of spreading God's Word to others, it was the person heading it that was a poor choice to her. Emery, a minister? Aimee had thought men of the cloth were supposed to act in utmost decorum and kindness. Emery did not seem to fit the part.

"Good afternoon, milady." A slightly accented voice chimed from behind her. Aimee did not recognize that voice, and she had been on this ship for quite a while. It was certainly too silky and refined to belong to Emery or any of his crew.

Aimee spun around and caught the gaze of one of the most exotically handsome men she had ever seen. Twinkling blue-green eyes lined with thick black lashes stood out on his handsomely etched face, contrasting his golden-bronzed skin. Black, corkscrew curls were swept back in a queue that seemed unfairly unaffected by the Caribbean summer breeze. He was richly dressed, a welcome sight to Aimee's eyes, and stood quite tall. She had never seen him on the *Cross's Victory* before, so what on earth was he doing here now?

"How could the captain have neglected introducing me to such a fair morsel?" The handsome man spanned the distance between them in two short steps, before snatching her hand and pressing the backs of her fingers to his lips. Aimee's face heated at his attention. "Eric Honeysett at your service, beautiful lady."

More than just the tropical sun caused sweat to form at Aimee's neck. She'd been on this ship for months now, and it had been so long since she'd received the attention of a gentleman. "Lady Aimee Dawson, sir." Only after she had introduced herself did Aimee realize that was no longer her name. No, she supposed she was now, "Aimee Emery." She hated the sound of that. Nonetheless, Aimee presented herself with her most welcoming curtsy as she tittered over the striking man's attention. "What are you doing with us on Emery's ship, Mr. Honeysett?"

"Ah, milady, it wounds me that the captain has not spoken of me to someone as beautiful as you." Mr. Honeysett's slight accent sounded distinctly French, and it warmed Aimee's heart, since her own mother was French. Aimee noted that the man continued to hold her hand in his, but she did not mind his touch. It offered a welcome diversion from her current prospects. "Captain Emery hired me as translator for his work in Haiti. I shall be sailing with you there. I hope you will not mind my company, mademoiselle."

* * *

For a reason he could not explain, when Matthew saw Aimee—the woman he despised most in the world—being touched by Eric Honeysett, his blood boiled, and his fists clenched at his sides. What bothered him even more was that Aimee did not recoil from the stranger's touch. No, the blasted woman seemed to relish it!

He watched as the man kissed her fingers once again. What was it with men's attraction to this little spitfire? Once they got to know her, they should be repulsed with her attitude. So why did it bother Matthew to see another man—a very good-looking man—touching her? Perhaps he felt this sudden protectiveness because she was his wife now. Yes, that must be it. He must have assumed some natural urge to guard her.

Matthew cleared his throat, causing Eric to jump backward and relinquish his hold on Aimee.

"Ah, how do you do, Captain?" Honeysett bowed low with a flourish of his arm.

"Excuse me, Mr. Honeysett, but I need to speak to my *wife* privately."

"This beautiful morsel is your wife, Captain? I had no idea. And you left her alone on this ship without a protector?" Mr. Honeysett stood up to his full height, an inch or so taller than Matthew, an attempt to intimidate him.

"Miss Daw—I mean, Mrs. Emery is perfectly capable of taking care of herself." Matthew placed his hand on Aimee's back. "Please excuse us while we speak in my—our cabin." Aimee reached behind her shoulder and grasped Matthew's

34

hand with hers. At first, he found the gesture endearing. Was she actually going to play along with their ruse of a marriage in front of this man?

But then, her nails dug into his skin so hard he almost yelped. "Emery, I do not think it is necessary for us to speak in private—"

"Woman, you will join me in our cabin immediately."

"A lover's quarrel? Perhaps I could talk to the lady for you, Captain, and clear things up on your behalf. I have always been a smashing success with the ladies."

Matthew decided to add Mr. Honeysett's cocky smirk to the growing list of reasons not to like the man. "No, Mr. Honeysett, you cannot talk to my wife for me. In fact, considering I am your employer, you would do well to remain outside of my personal affairs."

"I see." Honeysett caught Aimee's hand once more and drew it to his lips before striding away.

Matthew grabbed Aimee by the waist and tugged her in the direction of his cabin before she had a chance to realize what he was doing and stop him. By the time she started putting up a decent fight, they were already in his cabin and he had time to shut the door, lest she try to make an escape.

"Ugh, you beast!" she shouted when he blocked the door with his body. "What do you want with me?" Her slender finger poked him in the shoulder.

"I wish to have a civil conversation with my wife. In fact, I do not think we have ever shared a civil conversation together." Although, in his eyes, most of the negativity stemmed from Aimee, Matthew had to admit he had allowed their relationship to start off on the wrong foot from the first day they met. In an effort to calm the woman down, he placed a hand on her shoulder and gently nudged her away from the door.

Bad idea.

"Get your grimy, sailor hands off of me!" She exploded, shoving him away.

Matthew had a half a mind to tell her that she was the one to touch him first, but thought it wise to bite his tongue. Instead, he blurted, "Oh, you cannot possibly stand the touch of your own husband? You did not mind that stranger having his hands all over you." Matthew brushed his finger against a blond curl that had loosened from her updo, admittedly shocked at how soft it felt. The scent of lavender washed over him.

She had the audacity to laugh in his face as she swatted his hand away. "He by no means had his hands *all over me*. Mr. Honeysett was being a gentleman and introducing himself to me. Not that you would understand common etiquette, though—you should have introduced him to me from the start."

Matthew resisted the urge to growl. Surely Aimee had enough common sense to see that Mr. Honeysett was nothing but trouble? "Aimee, I said I would like to have a civil conversation with you about this. How about we sit down and enjoy a cup of tea?"

Aimee shook her head and rubbed her hands across her face. "All right. I will humor you this once."

"Good." The tea in the pot on his small table had chilled some since earlier this morning, but it would have to do. Matthew stepped across his cabin and gestured for her to sit. After she had settled, he lowered himself onto the chair across from her and poured her a cup of lukewarm tea. She scooped one, two, three spoonfuls of sugar and dumped them into her tea. She brought the cup to her lips and winced, no doubt at the temperature of the drink. Probably one more failure on his part in her eyes.

"So, why have you not introduced me to your newest crew member? What is Mr. Honeysett doing here?" Her teacup clattered as she rested it back on her saucer. She reached for the sugar and added another spoonful. Goodness, the woman consumed quite a bit of sugar for someone with such a sour personality!

"I hired Mr. Honeysett because I needed his services. He is fluent in French and can speak bits of the languages of the native people around here. In order to do some mission work I have been planning, I need help speaking the language of the people I hope to reach." Matthew sipped his lukewarm tea.

"How kind of him—to assist you in your mission work. I like him already." Aimee batted a stray curl out of her face. Her golden curls were just as rebellious as she was, it would seem.

"Aimee, I must ask you to avoid Mr. Honeysett. I am not certain what it is, but something about him sets me on edge. He does not seem to be a man who treats women how they should be treated, and I do not like to see him around you. He had his hands all over you and was taking too many liberties."

"He was simply acting like a gentleman, Matthew." She did a nice job at keeping her voice calm and even while disagreeing with him, he had to admit. If there was a profession in arguing, she would excel at it.

"A gentleman does not touch a woman...especially another man's *wife* for that long. I do not know what kind of *gentlemen* suitors you have had in the past, but that is not proper behavior." Matthew straightened his vest and narrowed his eyes at the woman. She harbored a lot of hatred in that little body of hers. Hatred directed mostly at him, of course. "While

Mr. Honeysett is with us, we need to make it clear to him that we are married so he understands that you are off-limits."

"Why on earth would we do that?" She scrunched up her pert little nose.

"Because, you are my wife, and I do not want him thinking you are available to him for the taking. And believe me, you do not want to get tangled up with a man like that." Matthew shuddered at the thought of any woman dealing with a man like Mr. Honeysett…Matthew had little respect for his own mother, but he remembered when unwanted suitors showed up on her doorstep and what the consequences were.

Aimee crossed her arms over her chest, and suddenly, Matthew found himself a tad bit distracted. What was wrong with him? He should not be attracted to this bratty, conceited woman. "So how do you plan on making it clear to Mr. Honeysett that we are married?"

* * *

Aimee resisted the urge to growl at Matthew. That would be far too unladylike of her to do. What was wrong with him? She was not *truly* his wife. Sure, he had mentioned making a promise to her at their rushed wedding, but surely he would consider that a matter of circumstance and end their marriage. She deserved the right to marry well and have children. Maybe Mr. Honeysett would be a good option for her. He was so handsome and he seemed so refined—like he knew the finer things in life and appreciated them, too.

Matthew inhaled deeply, and then exhaled. Inhaled again.

Exhaled again. Swallowed. Tightened his fingers into fists. Released them. Inhaled again. "I…I suppose you could…uh… *live* in here…with…me."

Now it was Aimee's turn to suck in a breath as it felt like her very life was tugged from her in that one sentence. If…if they consummated their marriage…whether they did so or it was assumed that they did…she would certainly bear a red mark if she got an annulment. She would never snag a decent, worthy husband. "I…I cannot do that, Matthew. Surely you know that."

"Yes, you can. You're my wife."

"It is plain to see that you did not want this marriage either, Matthew, so why go on with this charade? Why not pretend it never happened?" Aimee bit her lip as she waited for his response.

Mathew's jaw tightened, and he ran a hand through his hair. "Aimee. I will admit that I never wished for this marriage. Heaven knows, we are the last two people on earth our friends could see getting married to each other. But when I saw you up there, on that platform…with those men…I knew God had brought me there in that moment. I knew that, for whatever incomprehensible reason, He had those men force us to marry. He planned it. And when God plans something, it would be foolish to walk all over it or forget about it and disgrace it. I made a promise to you before God to protect you, and… and cherish you, and I…I don't hate you, Aimee. I've said it before, and I will say it as many times as I need to before you understand: I am not going to break my promise. I am not that kind of man. I may not love you; I may not get along with you, but I am going to give our marriage all my effort."

Aimee's chest tightened. Tears blurred her vision. Perhaps

he was right. Perhaps God *did* want them together. If that was so, then maybe God hated her. But should she give this marriage a chance? After all, she *had* made a promise, just like Matthew.

"I will live in this cabin with you, if you believe I must. But I will sleep on the cot. Alone."

Matthew's breathing slowed. He worked his jaw again. "All right. If that's what the princess demands, then so be it."

Aimee tried to stop her face from drawing up into a frown. The voice of her mother echoed in her head. *Ladies do not frown. It could create wrinkles.* "Would you please stop calling me princess? I beg of you."

Matthew grinned saucily. The act was so unlike him, Aimee had to blink twice to be sure she was not going insane. "I don't think I should make any more promises to you, milady."

* * *

Matthew had to admit, he did not expect to see a small smile upturn Aimee's rosy lips.

"Well, should we see about getting your things transferred to my cabin?" He offered his arm for her to take, and worked to disguise a gasp when, after a moment, she took his arm.

"I hope you do not have a rat problem in your room." She sniffed as the stepped into the companionway.

Matthew threw his head back and laughed. The lady actually had a sense of humor! She, of course, was referring to the time a month ago, when she claimed to have been terrorized by a rat that entered her cabin. Matthew sobered a little bit when he recalled how cruel he had been to her in those days, but truly, she deserved it. There was no reason to be so irrationally afraid of a tiny rodent!

Aimee tugged her hand away from him and rested it on her chest. "I don't think it was a laughing matter."

Matthew squeezed his eyes shut and inhaled before responding, "Aimee, I do not know why we are always at odds with each other. Like I have said, I will admit that I am not completely fond of you, but that does not mean we have to be at each other's throats for the rest of our lives."

"I grow weary of this conversation as well. Can't we just be? Must we be constantly evaluating how we treat each other?" She slid her hand from her chest, down her waist and to her shapely hip, drawing Matthew's attention down there. He shook his head. This woman was an expert at getting what she wanted, and she knew how to use whatever methods she needed to get it—even if that meant flirting with a man she had no feelings for. Matthew used to know a woman just like her, and he was not stupid enough to get his heart hurt by such a woman again.

"C'mon, princess. Let's get your things and move you to our cabin."

Chapter 4

A squeak reverberated across every fiber of the cabin. Aimee tucked her legs onto the cot and squeezed her eyes shut. If that was a rat, she did not want to see it. Anything that crawled around in the slime of the bottom of the boat was not something Aimee wanted to encounter. *Please go away, please go away.*

A knock sounded. The cabin door creaked open. Aimee squeezed her eyes shut even tighter and tried to make herself as still as possible. She did not need Matthew to see her afraid of another rat.

"Well, what is this?"

Aimee pried her eyes open. "Oh!" That wasn't Mr. Perfect's voice. It was…the man who was a whole lot more perfect than her husband. "What…what are you doing in here, Mr. Honeysett?" She stepped off of the cot and straightened her dress.

"Well, you are a lovely vision, Lady…*Emery*. I was here to find your husband, but obviously he is not here." Despite his words, Mr. Honeysett did not seem to be going anywhere else anytime soon. "I can see the captain was careless enough to leave you alone once again, my dear. You see, if you were mine, I would never let you out of my sight." Mr. Honeysett pressed a kiss to the back of her hand and peered into her eyes. "I am not sure that a man like him deserves a woman like you."

Aimee's face heated at his attention, however forward he was being for someone who barely knew her. If only she were not already married to Matthew... "Well, sir, is there anything I can do for you in lieu of my husband?"

"I would love the honor of your company for a few moments. You seem a fascinating woman. It is such a shame that your husband keeps you locked up in here for no one else to see."

"I suppose a little company couldn't hurt." Aimee motioned to the sole chair in the room, as she lowered herself back onto the cot.

"I beg you to tell me, mademoiselle, how a lady such as you has made it all the way to the Caribbean, and is the wife of a mere merchant? I can sense an air of refinement from you. You must not be from this area originally."

Aimee fluffed her pink skirt around her body on the cot. This dress needed a reprieve and a good washing, but she had only been able to take a small portion of her wardrobe on her trip. "You are correct, sir. I was born and raised in London. I come from a wealthy family, a well-known family back in England."

"And your father allowed your marriage to a simple merchantman?" Mr. Honeysett opened his stance and leaned closer.

"Well...my father does not know about the marriage yet. He will find out soon enough."

"Oh? Is it that recent? You know, a gentleman would have asked your father for your hand in marriage."

"Matthew did not have an opportunity to ask my father, as we just got married yesterday."

"Yesterday? Well, congratulations, newlywed."

* * *

Eric Honeysett observed as the lady blushed prettily, the pink just staining her cheeks the perfect amount to become her even more, without turning overly red. Yes, she was a pretty one. Although Eric always told himself he should stop his womanizing ways, he decided this one would be his last. She was too enchanting to resist! Besides, she was connected to a lot of money back in England. She would be a great asset to him. And it looked like she was falling right into his charms.

"Aimee…may I call you that? Aimee?" He gently took her hand in his. It felt smooth and soft, as a woman's hand should. It was lacking gloves, but he assumed she had given up on them after being in the Caribbean for a while.

Aimee's gaze shot to the door, as if waiting for her husband to walk in on them. It would not be the first time a husband walked in on Eric and his latest conquest, but he was always successful in defending himself. Besides, he enjoyed living an unpredictable life.

"It's all right. Don't you worry."

"I…I suppose it would not hurt anyone if you called me Aimee."

"Good. Now, Aimee, I was wondering whether you had a proper wedding."

"A proper wedding?"

"Why, of course. A beautiful bride like you deserves dancing and food and a lot of attention." Eric stood and started pacing the room, as if her rushed wedding was the biggest injustice of the century. "I think at the least, a well-wishing good luck kiss is in order for the bride, my dear."

Aimee jolted from the cot, eyes wide. "Why, sir, we have just met. I believe that is a little out of line. Besides, I am a married woman."

"Oh, sweet thing, you misjudge me. It is customary for the bride to receive a kiss on the cheek from those around her at her wedding."

A wrinkle creased her brow. "All right, I suppose, if it is a tradition. A kiss on the cheek." Her eyes slid closed, eyelashes fluttering.

Eric had to contain a laugh of excitement. This girl was almost pathetic in her yearning for attention. She would be easy to sway toward him, especially because she did not seem to get along with her new husband well. Perhaps Captain Emery had trapped her into this marriage somehow. Eric could almost see himself in charge of her wealthy estate, living back in London or maybe even France, the land of his father. If Eric believed in such things, he would say this woman was an answer to a prayer!

Eric waited to approach her until he felt the ship rise up on the crest of a wave. At the perfect moment, Eric leaned forward as if to brush his lips against her cheek. The force of the wave they drifted over allowed Eric to dramatize their shifting balance so he could miss her cheek and snag her lips instead. He lingered there for a moment and grabbed her shoulders in a showy effort to stabilize her. Finally, she seemed to realize what was happening and tore away from him. Her hands flew to cover her mouth as she stepped away.

Perhaps he had acted a little too quickly. Well, it would not be difficult to play that off as an accident to her. She may be pretty, but she did not seem to have a lot of activity in her head.

"I beg you, mademoiselle, forgive me. I lost my balance when we surged over that wave. What just happened was never my intention."

The door creaked open. Captain Emery sauntered in and seemed to assess the situation. Eric had seen this happen before. The captain loped over to Aimee and encircled her in his arm. She didn't seem to know whether to lean into her husband's embrace or draw away. That was good for Eric. It proved he had a chance with her. She might not have admitted why she was married to this man that she did not seem so fond of, but Eric could tell she would not regret leaving him overly much.

"What was never your intention, Mr. Honeysett?" Captain Emery pulled Aimee a little closer to his side, purposely making eye contact with Eric as he did so.

"It was never my intention to…find her alone. I was searching for you, sir." He winked at the lady.

* * *

Mathew pushed the door closed behind Mr. Honeysett on his way out. "What did that man do to you, Aimee?" He stepped closer to his wife. Her little hands covered her mouth. Her sparkling green eyes were huge, and her cheeks were flushed pink. She shook her head furiously.

"Aimee, obviously something happened while I was away."

Aimee seemed to realize the position of her hands and dropped them to her sides, before promptly raising them to fiddle with a lock of her hair obsessively. "It is none of your business. Please, you have no reason to be interested."

When would the woman understand that he had promised his life to her? Whether or not he liked it, he had vowed to protect this woman. And, protecting her heart from nefarious men who only cared about her pleasing looks was part of his duty. Matthew may never truly like his wife, but God had made her his for some reason, and he wanted to puzzle that out sooner rather than later.

"Aimee. Please understand that I have your best interest at heart. Mr. Honeysett is a dangerous man, and I do not like to see you cavorting with him, my dear princess."

Much to his dismay, defiance re-lit her eyes. "I was not *cavorting* with Mr. Honeysett."

Her fury always seemed to get Matthew even more riled up. She did not seem able to discern what was good for her and what was not. It was about time he scared her into behaving a little bit more respectfully. "Oh yes? What happened, then?" He grabbed her upper arms and drew her up against him. "Did he do this?" Matthew pulled her closer still, and crushed her lips with his. "Is this what had you so flustered, so pink in the face? Is this what you like a man to do to you?" He kissed her again, hard and unrelenting.

She pushed her hands against his chest and he immediately allowed her to free herself, ice running in his veins at the realization of what he had just done.

"What is *wrong* with you, Emery?" Aimee scrubbed her hands against her face, gasping for breath. "You...you had no permission to kiss me!"

"Mr. Honeysett has permission to kiss you, then? And your husband does not?"

"Eric had no permission. He told me it was an accident. He lost his balance when we sailed over some choppy water." Aimee turned her head to the side so she did not have to see him as she spoke, and he wondered if she truly believed that falsehood.

Matthew released her with a laugh at how ridiculous she was. "All right, princess. If you are addle-brained enough to believe that tale, I will not stop you. But I do ask you to refrain from kissing any other men. I am here to protect you, princess. And men like him are dangerous to you and to your reputation."

"Matthew, I am a woman grown. I do not have to succumb to your will. Mr. Honeysett is a gentleman." The lady sank down onto the cot, a horrified look still darkening her face.

Anger boiled deep inside Matthew. This woman would be the death of him. Why must she be so stubborn?

"All right, Aimee. I can see that I am getting nowhere with you. But I sincerely hope you will have a change of heart. As the ward of your pastor back in England, I want you to know that kissing a man other than your husband is not right."

With that, Matthew pulled the door open and slammed it behind him. He leaned back against the door and his eyes slid shut. He had no idea why God had tossed him and Aimee together, but Matthew had a feeling that living with this woman was about to be the largest test of his life.

* * *

Aimee touched the doorknob that her husband had just touched. Was there something wrong with her, that Matthew would never like her? She had never asked for Eric to kiss her, never wanted him to kiss her. Goodness! She had pulled away as soon as she had realized what the man was doing. So why did Matthew have to make such a fuss about it?

Her lips still burned from Matthew's touch. For someone she disliked so much, his kiss had pleasantly affected her. What was wrong with her?

Aimee stepped away from the door. She was going to attempt to get along more pleasantly with Matthew. She simply needed to put forth some effort. Maybe she should clean up his cabin. He would probably be happy with that. A glance around told her that he did not need his cabin straightened up. Everything was perfect. No matter, she would find something she could do to make this cabin more welcoming.

Papers were lined up perfectly on his desk. A teacup rested perpendicular to them, its contents chilled. A quill pen lay aligned with an inkpot, all neatly placed. What would he do if something was displaced? It might irk him to no end. Sadly, Aimee had told herself she would not upset the dolt any further.

Aimee noted the cover to the inkwell was resting crooked in the pot. Finally, something Aimee could fix. She snatched up the inkwell and tried to pop the cover off, but it was stuck. Perhaps the ink had dried to the surface, and was making it more difficult to open. Aimee stepped toward the other end of the desk, closer to the light pouring through the porthole, and gave the lid a yank. The inkwell seemed to jump from her hands of its own volition and clatter onto the desk, its cover in Aimee's grip. Black ink dripped out of the pot and straight onto the papers adorning Matthew's desk. *Blast.*

"Oh no, no, no!" Aimee plucked her lavender-scented, perfectly pink handkerchief from her shirtwaist and tried to soak up the ink. Half the inkwell's contents had poured out over Matthew's documents. Maybe he would not notice?

Aimee did her best to clean up the mess, but unfortunately, several of the papers seemed beyond repair. Matthew was going to hate her even more now but maybe, if she buried the damaged documents underneath some untarnished papers, it would delay them being discovered. There, that was settled. Aimee would hate to give cause for Matthew to be cross with her. So, she would have to make sure that the rest of the cabin was in perfect order. The room was far too unwelcoming. It was too dark, too orderly, and too plain. Aimee knew the perfect addition to this dull cabin. She snatched her pink quilt from her bag and strew it across the cot. There—that added a little bit of color to the room, and filled the air with her favorite scent: lavender. The cabin already looked much nicer. Next, Aimee waited for her ink-drenched handkerchief to dry before using it to dust Matthew's desk, not that there *was* any dust covering it. Aimee straightened out her quilt to make the cot look even more orderly. She just happened to have some of her lacework with her, so she artfully placed doilies and coverings around the room and the desk. This place needed a woman's touch. Even Matthew would be happy with her attention to detail. Maybe he would look at her with something other than disgust for once in his life.

Before Matthew returned, Aimee decided it would also be good if she looked her best, too. She pulled out her small hand mirror and applied a light coloring of rouge to her lips and cheeks. A few hairpins helped neaten her updo. When she was finished, Aimee had to admit she felt just a little pride in herself for her fresh idea to impress her husband.

Chapter 5

⚜

O ne night. One more night, and they would make shore on the island that Matthew could not wait to visit. A missionary friend of Reverend Dobb's had alerted him of the native and mixed peoples on this island who were in need of religious aid. Matthew had been more than happy to oblige, while he awaited for the final portion of his merchant order to be filled back in Port Royal. He could not wait to preach the Good News to native people who may have never heard of it before, as well as to help them and tend to their sick. Being a preacher was what Matthew knew he was born to do, and he could not wait to do some of his future work right now.

He would just have to deal with his stubborn, snooty little wife for one night before he could be doing what he loved. One night…alone with his wife. In his cabin. Matthew gulped. He was not looking forward to being trapped in such a confined space with that woman. So, he delayed his return to his cabin as late as he could.

Unfortunately, nighttime hit, and Matthew found himself waiting in front of his door. Should he knock? Was that what a married man did? He did not want to startle his new wife. Matthew raised a fist to knock, but the door opened before he made contact with it. Aimee greeted him with a warm smile, something Matthew had rarely seen from her before, especially when in such close proximity.

"Good evening, Matthew. Do you care to have a cup of tea with me?"

A darker pink than usual stained her cheeks, and her lips were a gorgeous shade of red. Golden-blond hair was swept backward in beautiful curls. The fresh scent of lavender tickled his nose. She was up to some mischief, and Matthew had no care to find out what it was. However, she was being kind to him, and he also had no intention of discouraging that.

"I would love to join you for a cup of tea, Aimee. Care to let me into *your* cabin?" Matthew studied her as she flashed him a brilliant smile, opened the door further, and motioned for him to enter.

The entire cabin smelled like her. Lavender. Lavender, everywhere. It was a lovely scent, but if Matthew spent much time in here, he might just emerge smelling like a girl. There was no doubt his crew would have a wonderful time teasing him about that.

The contents of his desk were arranged in a slightly different pattern than the way he had left them. That was the first thing he noticed about the room, besides the feminine smell. A teapot, steaming hot, sat on his desk, along with some teacups and saucers as well. Matthew did not have the heart to tell her that the tea set had come from the stock that he was supposed to return to London.

Aimee moved over toward the cot. A flash of color caught Matthew's eye. Pink. He craned his neck to see past his wife. "What's that?"

"Oh, that's just my quilt. I thought the room needed some color. Everything was so dark and dull." The woman had brought her quilt from home? No wonder she carried so many bags with her. He supposed he had never told her he disliked the color pink. Aimee dumped sugar by the spoonful into her tea. Maybe Matthew should stop allowing tea onboard if his wife was going to use up their entire supply of sugar in one cup of tea.

"Pink?"

She cast him a sheepish smile through her eyelashes. "It was all I had. I assumed that because I was going to be the one occupying the cot, you would not mind the color of the quilt I used. I do get cold, anyway, you know. I like to have an extra blanket."

Matthew had to bite his tongue to keep from calling her a spoiled princess. However, he had decided that he was going to get along more pleasantly with his wife, and she hated it when he called her a princess. "Well, I have no objection to allowing you to stay warm, milady. However, when my crew comes in here, I would appreciate the blanket to be out of the way. They would never let me hear the end of it. A pink blanket." He shook his head. This woman was daft.

"Oh, I apologize, Emery. I was trying to make this room more cheerful. It needed a woman's touch, I think. Of course, if I were back home, I would have a multitude of decorations to add to the place, but those will have to wait."

Matthew had to bite back a grin. She was kind of charming as she chattered on. However, as Matthew had experience with a woman much like her, he knew her charm was just that—charm. Something fake. A show put on to trick a poor fool like him into doing whatever she wanted. No matter how unnatural it seemed to not be fighting with her, however, he was not going to do so. "Of course, Aimee. I will allow you to decorate however you wish." Matthew sipped his tea.

"Thank you. I appreciate it." Aimee rested her hand on his arm lightly.

Matthew shifted, still a little bit uncomfortable with her sudden attention. "Yes. Well…" He gulped down the rest of his tea, "I apologize if I am imposing on you, but I am afraid I am terribly tired. Would you mind if I retired early?"

A slight shadow crossed her features. "Of course not. I suppose I am feeling a little bit sleepy, as well." Aimee rose. "I am sleeping on the cot, right?"

Matthew sighed. Like there had been any choice on his part. "Correct, milady. It would not be right to ask you to sleep on the floor."

"I…I apologize that I am not sharing the cot, and I feel terrible for making you sleep on the floor while I am comfortable, but…but…" Her face reddened, and her fingers twisted in her hands. "But, you understand. I am just not ready, and—"

Matthew caught her hand and stilled it. "I understand. Stay on the cot. I will not bother you." He feared he looked entirely too eager to arrange a few blankets and a pillow as far away from the cot as he could get them.

"Thank you, Emery." Aimee remained upright on the cot as Matthew curled up on the deck floor. It was hard and uncomfortable, and reminded Matthew of the many nights he had spent sleeping on the floor of his mother's room before Reverend Dobbs had taken him in. Unexpectedly, a wave of grief for his lost childhood washed over him. He resisted the urge to groan. He had not felt that sadness for years… why, practically since he had been abandoned by his mother. Matthew hated to feel pity for himself. He was a grown man, and those days were behind him.

"Emery?"

Matthew scrubbed his face with his hands. If she was going to ask him what was wrong, he would not be able to talk about it. It was none of her business! He doused the lantern that lit the cabin, hoping that would make his wife realize that he did not wish to speak.

"Emery?"

No such luck. "Yes, Aimee, what is it?"

"Are you all right?"

No.

Her bare feet padded toward him.

Maybe if he closed his eyes, she would think he was asleep already. Since when did she care about him, anyway?

A soft, warm hand rested on his temple, brushing a lock of hair away from his face. "Emery?"

Matthew took a moment to breathe before opening his eyes and responding. "Yes, *darling*?" He used the affectionate term sarcastically, but immediately regretted it. Aimee, however, did not seem to notice. She was too busy boring into his soul with her emerald-green eyes.

* * *

Aimee brushed her hand against Matthew's cheek. He may be pretending that nothing was wrong, but she had seen the shadow of anguish that had darkened his face before he extinguished the light in the cabin. Something was upsetting him, and Aimee wanted to know what it was. His earlier words had hit her. Maybe she was stuck with him for the rest of their lives. She should try to comfort him. Isn't that what a good wife would do? Maybe whatever had him upset was also making him angry at her. Besides, she had seen kindness in him, just from the way he interacted with everyone but her. If only she were a little more kind to him, maybe they could get along. She leaned closer. Moonlight from the porthole just above him illuminated his face. His eyes were red, and sad. Was he about to cry?

"Emery. Are you all right?"

"Goodness, did you not understand when I said I wished to retire for the night?" He snagged her wrist gently and drew her hand away from his face.

"I understood what you said. I was concerned for you." She pulled against his grasp, but he kept her wrist there, close to his chest as if he did not really want to let her go. She was amazed at how she didn't mind being this close to him. She took a moment to appreciate how handsome he was, with his tan skin and deep blue eyes.

"Aimee, I appreciate your concern. But I do not want to talk about it. I remembered something foolish, and it should not have bothered me as it did just now. Forget about it. Do you understand?"

Tears filled Aimee's eyes. The one time she worried about him, the one time she expressed a shred of care, he brushed her aside. "I understand, Emery. I'm sorry to have bothered you." Aimee retracted, this time snatching her hand free. "Goodnight, then."

"Goodnight, Aimee." Emery's reply reached her just as she reclined back on the cot.

She closed her eyes tight, trying to think of something to do, something to say to get to the bottom of this. But it was best not to start an argument.

Aimee supposed she would have to change into her nightgown here, in front of Emery. It was dark, though, so he would not see her. Nevertheless, she should warn him. "I must change into my nightgown. Would you please turn your back?"

Emery didn't make a noise, but turned to the side.

Aimee still struggled to unfasten the back of her dress, but she had grown more accustomed to changing without help while Ivy was away. Oh, she wondered how that sweet girl was doing. After they had set out on an expedition to find their friend, Eden, Ivy had decided to part ways in Port Royal. She was heading back toward England, with a week or so head start on Aimee and Matthew. She had joined Captain Gage Thompson, the friend of Eden's husband. Aimee could not wait to see her wise friend and talk to her about the awful situation she had gotten herself into. Ivy would know what to do. Unfortunately, Ivy would probably advise her to remain married to Emery. Oh, the misfortune! She sighed as she pulled her pink nightgown over her head. It would seem that there was no way out of her situation as Emery's wife. *Please, God, make this more bearable. I know that I have been selfish in the past, and have been more than a little irritable when it comes to Emery, but please do not make the rest of my life unbearable. I will try my hardest to get along with my husband.*

Aimee undid her hair from its updo and braided it to prevent tangles. Finally, she was ready to go to bed. "I'm finished dressing, Emery."

Emery did not make a sound, but rolled over onto his back.

She resisted the urge to grumble. It did not look like she would be falling asleep any time soon. Aimee had never slept with a man in the room before. Every slight movement he made on the floor, just feet away from her, seemed to explode in her ears. His deep breathing was a new sound to her. His masculine cedar scent filled the air, nearly overpowering her beloved lavender. Aimee tucked herself further into the bed, pulling her pink quilt up to her chin.

She prayed that after tonight, she would grow accustomed to this situation, because if she did not, she could be looking forward to a lifetime of no sleep.

* * *

Emery awoke on the unforgiving deck of his cabin. His shoulder was killing him from the position he had slept in. He opened an eye and glanced around. Sunlight streamed in, signifying that he had slept far later than he had ever intended to sleep. Perhaps that was because he could barely stay asleep with the rock-hard deck beneath him.

He leapt up and folded his blankets. The noise must have stirred Aimee, for she rolled over toward his direction, groaning and draping her arm over the edge of the cot. She certainly was pretty when she was asleep. Her golden-blond hair once was confined into a braid over her shoulder, but now the majority of it was loose and dancing around her cheek with every bounce of a wave. Her dark lashes tickled her creamy, white skin, and the edges of her pink lips were tilted upward. It was quite rare for Emery to see a smile on that pretty face of hers. However, it was well past dawn, and time for the both of them to be awake, so Emery would have to disturb her sooner or later, and a frown would soon cross her expression.

"Aimee," he whispered. She did not stir. "Aimee!" he shook her shoulders.

Her green eyes immediately opened, as wide as saucers. After a second, they narrowed. "What do you want?" She slapped his hands away as she turned onto her side.

"I don't want anything. I just wanted to let you know how late it is. I assumed you would want to be up by now." Matthew leaned down to push a lock of hair out of her face.

"Oh. Well, you might as well have allowed me to sleep. I did not even blink last night. I am lucky if I slept for five minutes! Besides, I have nowhere to be besides this wretched ship. What does it matter if I sleep longer?" Her pretty emerald eyes drifted shut as she spoke.

"Oh. Well, I am sorry you did not get much sleep last night, Aimee. I thought you would be more comfortable on the bed than on the floor." Matthew resisted the urge to roll his eyes at her nonsense.

She didn't respond, but pulled the covers closer to her chin and seemed to completely drift off to sleep. Matthew had never seen anything like it! Well, he supposed she would get up on her own at some point, so he decided to just leave her be as she was.

Matthew ran a comb through his hair and straightened his clothes before heading onto the main deck. The cool sea breeze hit him the moment he stepped out, and he felt a smile upturn his lips.

It was well past dawn, and the bright sky seemed an even deeper blue than ever before. Turquoise waters slapped against the hull of the ship as they sailed. A seabird soared above him, softly cawing. He was glad they had just missed a hurricane that had passed, and they were left with the beautiful sea as he knew it.

Goodness, he had never been so relieved to leave his cabin before. It had been absolute torture to sleep in the same cabin as that woman. Until a few days ago, he had never thought he would ever sleep so close to her…or be her *husband*!

"Heavenly Father, you work in mysterious ways. Please help me understand what you are doing here." Matthew looked upward as he spoke. He almost feared his marriage was some mistake, but he knew that with God, there were no mistakes.

"Who were you speaking to, Captain?"

The one man Matthew did not want to see sauntered up to him, a suspicious grin on his face. Eric Honeysett crossed his arms as he approached and then leaned against the rail of the ship casually.

"I was not speaking to you, sir."

His eyebrows shot up to nearly his hairline. "I apologize, Captain. It seemed as though you were speaking to the air."

"I was praying. Not that it concerned you at all, Honeysett."

A smirk crossed his face. "Well, some might still consider that you were indeed speaking to the air."

Why on earth had this man agreed to help Matthew translate for his missionary work if he said such things? However, he decided to let the comment slide. There was something else he wished to discuss with the man.

"Mr. Honeysett, I do need to speak with you."

"Yes, Captain? Whatever about?"

Matthew shifted his balance. "Well, Mr. Honeysett, it is about my wife."

"Ah, Captain, you need some advice on what to do with her, huh? I heard you were married this week. Tell me, did she not satisfy you last night?" He wiggled his eyebrows at him.

"Mr. Honeysett, I am appalled that you would speak of my wife in such a crude manner. I expect to hear nothing so foul out of your mouth again." Since when was Matthew so protective of the sassy little woman? He supposed since he became her husband. "Now, while we are on the topic of my wife...I said I need to speak with you about her." Matthew inhaled. He was never one to directly confront someone he had an issue with. Granted, he always had addressed matters when they needed addressing, but he never particularly enjoyed it. He clenched his fists. "I know what you did to my wife yesterday. She told me everything. I expect you to leave her alone. I never want you to lay a hand on her again."

"I apologize, Captain, if she accepts affection from me and not from you. You see, I have always had a way with ladies. They adore me. It is not my fault if your wife cannot keep her hands off of me."

Matthew clenched his jaw and resisted the urge to raise his fists. He knew Aimee. She may be silly, and she may be conceited, but she was not a woman who could not keep her hands off of a man she had merely just met. And Matthew would not tolerate a man who said otherwise. "Eric Honeysett, if you were an intelligent man, you would get off of my ship *right now*." Matthew had never resorted to violence, but right now he felt a whole lot like resorting to violence.

For a moment, something similar to fear flashed in Honeysett's eyes. It was soon replaced by defiance. "I have nowhere to go, Captain. Besides, you know you need a translator. You would not be able to do your *missionary* work without me to translate for you. You need me."

Although Matthew was practically dying to punch this man, he did use his brain before swinging his fists. Honeysett was a few inches taller, and a little bulkier as well. This would not be a fight in which Matthew would come out victorious. "Mr. Honeysett, if you speak about *my wife* in such a manner ever again, you will regret ever learning how to speak. Do you understand me, man?"

Mr. Honeysett looked him up and down, a wry grin on his face, as if he was showing just how unafraid of Matthew he was. "Very well, *Captain.*"

Matthew could not help but notice how unapologetic Honeysett appeared. There was nothing he could do about it, though, at least not at this time. "And I do not expect to hear you speaking about my wife in such a manner to anyone else, either. You hear me?"

"Yes, Captain."

"Good. Now go and make yourself useful. We will make land sometime soon in Hispaniola, and I want you to be prepared to work when we do."

"Matthew?" A soft hand rested on his arm. He spun around to find Aimee behind him. Her hair was still haphazardly restrained by a braid, but she had changed back into her fluffy, pink dress. Sleep still was evident on her face, and her eyelids drooped a little bit.

"What is it, *dear*?"

"Oh." Her eyes latched onto Mr. Honeysett and she froze,

something akin to fear darkening her eyes for a split second.

"Mr. Honeysett, you are excused."

"All right. Good morning, lovely Mrs. Emery. I hope to catch up with you later." The man stepped far too close to Aimee as he walked by her, lingering near her for a second.

Matthew wanted to lunge at him and tell him that he was behaving deplorably, but Aimee was not aware of their recent talk, and she did not need to be, either.

"Good day, sir," Aimee muttered well after the man had passed her and was on his way.

"What did you want, Aimee? I thought you had decided to sleep awhile longer?" Matthew turned to face his wife head-on.

"Oh, well, I seem to have forgotten what I came out here to ask you about. I am sorry about that. Was I interrupting something?" She seemed to notice the state of her hair and frantically attempted to wrangle it, but gave up when she only located a sole hairpin. Matthew hated to admit that he admired the way the blond locks reflected strands of gold and honey in the sunlight. Her hair was beautiful. Not that he intended to notice such things about her.

"Matthew?"

Oh, she had distracted him with her pretty hair. "No, no, you were not interrupting anything. I was discussing a matter with Mr. Honeysett, but it was settled by the time you arrived."

"Oh, I understand." She twisted a lock of that hair around her hand. Matthew had to look away, because his sudden feelings of not-hate toward her were frightening him quite a bit.

"When are we due to arrive at that island you were planning on visiting?"

"Oh, I would say we will arrive either tonight or first thing tomorrow. I have not been able to check my charts lately, but

I can tell we are close," Matthew said.

"And, would you mind explaining to me, what exactly you plan on doing at the island?" She continued to wind the hair around her hand.

"Well, I actually told you about my plans in Hispaniola, but back then, you were too cross with me to even listen to a word I said." Matthew chuckled ruefully. He had told her about what they were going to do—back on their wedding day. Goodness, that day seemed like a year ago, but it was only two days behind them.

"I…I am sorry about the way I used to treat you, Emery. I know that we don't get along very well, but I regret how often I was rude to you in the past." The woman bit her bottom lip as she spoke, drawing his attention there for a moment. She was a distracting little thing. Matthew allowed his mind to drift, to wonder what it would be like if she was a sweeter, kinder woman who actually liked him. He supposed he would like her, also, and then he might have a real marriage.

Matthew had never planned to get married. It would be nice to have a sweet, godly woman by his side, and some children running around in his name, but that was not Matthew's main goal. He did not need a woman by any means. From his experience, a lot of women were like his mother. And a woman like that was not something he needed in his life.

However, when Aimee smiled up at him so prettily, Matthew was almost happy he had become a married man. What was happening to him?

"Matthew, I said I was sorry." Wait, why was a frown forming on her brow? Oh, she was speaking to him. Matthew needed to stop allowing himself to get distracted. "I guess that what I do is never enough, then. I will never be good enough for you to look at me without hating me. I understand. I'm sorry that I am such a pain to you."

"Aimee, I never said anything like that about you." Blast, he had just defended this woman, and now she thought he hated her. What had he done wrong?

"I know you have not said anything, but I can tell how you feel by the way you act. Do you know how many times I have spoken to you, and you have ignored me in the last few days?" Her little hands were wound up into fists, and she defiantly placed them at her hips. Pink stained her cheeks and her green eyes flashed at him from under thick lashes.

Matthew needed to stop her before she got even angrier at him. He did not need to live with her in his cabin when she was killing mad. "Aimee, come with me. We need to talk."

She stood there glaring. "Why do we need to go somewhere else to talk?"

He gently gripped her shoulder and tried to nudge her back toward their cabin. She resisted and even slapped at his hand. "Aimee, dear, I am beginning to lose my patience. I beg you, come to my cabin so we can speak to each other. Privately. We do not need my crew listening in on us, and we need to speak. So let us do so from the privacy of our cabin."

Aimee rolled her eyes and started walking in the opposite direction, much like a disobedient puppy Matthew had once owned.

"Aimee!" Matthew lunged forward and caught her by the elbow. This time, she did not try to squirm out of his grasp immediately. At least that was a good sign, he supposed.

She looked back at him over her shoulder with a glare that could probably start a fire if she wanted.

"Come along, dear. I want to speak with you."

With a huff, she placed her hand atop his on her elbow. Matthew had learned his lesson before and snatched his fingers away before she could claw him with her fingernails. He grimaced at the memory of her talon-like nails. Those were a weapon just as effective as any sword or pistol.

* * *

Aimee squeezed her eyes shut and inhaled deeply. No matter how much she wanted to throw a tantrum and slam the door in Emery's face, she would behave like a grown, proper lady and not entertain her desires to express her unhappiness. She bit her lip and stepped through the threshold. Emery trailed closely and shut the door behind them once he stepped inside the room. He ran his hands through his hair and stood there looking at her for a few moments in complete silence.

Aimee raised her eyebrows. "You said you wish to speak to me, Emery, so speak."

"Yes." He took a step closer to her. "Aimee. I tried to leave all harsh feelings I've ever had for you back in the tavern when we got married that day. We have already had a few discussions about this. I want us to get along. I have been trying to be more kind to you, and I can see that you are making an effort to do the same."

Obviously she was! How could he not see all she had done for him, all of the times she had held back her temper when he made her upset? This man never failed to make her frustrated. And now, when it seemed they were just beginning to get along civilly, Emery had to go ahead and ruin it. Stupid man.

"You were not even listening to me, Emery. You had stopped paying attention. I made an effort to get along with you. I even cleaned your cabin for you. And how do you repay me? You try to forget that I exist." Aimee crossed her arms across her chest as pure anger bubbled up inside. She wanted to scream.

Emery seemed to share her sentiment, as he groaned and threw his hands in the air. "Aimee, I never did anything like that!"

Aimee found it more and more difficult to control herself. Blast, this man had seen her lose her temper before, so what did it matter if he saw her have a fit again? Tears found their way out of her eyes as she tried to keep her voice at an even tone. "I know what I saw, Emery." How dare he say she was lying? He made her want to hit him. Smack him with her fan right across his stupid, handsome face. He deserved it.

"I think I would know what I did more than you would know what you saw, *sweetheart.*"

"Oh, Matthew, stop it!" Aimee swung her hand up to slap him, but he caught her wrist first. She tried to hit him with her other hand, but at that point she was too distracted by the tears pouring out of her eyes to see him grab that hand, too. Was this to be the rest of her life? Constantly fighting with her husband, besides the occasional seconds when they got along? That seemed to be no way to live. There was no part of this marriage that was agreeable to Aimee, and she did not want to be dragged into it until death.

She fought against his grip, but he refused to lessen his hold on her. "Emery, let me go! Stop it!" She twisted, but he still held steady.

"Aimee, you are going to hurt yourself if you keep struggling.

I want to talk, and I want you to be still."

"No, I don't want to listen to you!" Aimee cringed at how whiny her voice sounded, but she could not stop. She also could not stop the tears from streaming down her cheeks.

"Come on."

The tears streamed down her face in sheets like the heaviest April rain. Aimee knew she looked like a blubbering idiot, and that made her even more upset with this dolt. He never failed to make her look her worst and humiliate herself. She shoved against his arms, although she knew that he was stronger than her by far.

"Stop fighting me." Matthew nudged her backward until she was flat against the bulkhead, and she still struggled. "Aimee." He moved his grip on her so his arms were wrapped around her in a tight embrace, rather than blatantly restraining her. She gave up on the fight at that point, knowing he would win anyway. Besides, there was a strange pleasantness to be held in his arms. She felt safe, even when five days ago, she never would have imagined such a thing to be possible. The tears flowed even more freely now, and she rested her cheek against his chest. He patted her on the shoulder and seemed to accept that she just needed to cry for a few moments. His hand moved up to the back of her neck and got tangled up in her hair. He left it there, gently massaging her neck as she cried and cried until the tears slowed. Although Aimee had just been horribly angry with this man, here he was comforting her and making her feel safe. "Aimee, you do not need to cry. Just breathe. I want to talk to you and say something that I should have said years ago."

Aimee bit her lip and scrunched her face up in an attempt to stop crying. "Go…ahead." She hated the gasping way she spoke. She sounded like a child right now.

"I want to be civil to you. I want us to get along. I want us to make this marriage work. We cannot be fighting every five minutes, sweetheart. Now, I would never purposely ignore you. I admit, I let my mind wander a few times, but when I did, I was thinking about…about…"

"What? What were you thinking about?" Aimee sniffled as she rubbed her cheek against Matthew's shoulder in an attempt to dry it. She would have rubbed her cheek with her hands, but he held her tight as chains in his arms. She craned her neck back in an effort to look at his expression. His lips were set into a tight line, and he stared down at her. Suddenly, she was very much aware of how close she was to this man.

Shadows crossed his expression as he thought. Finally, he spoke. "Aimee, I was thinking about you. I know this is a blasted foolish thing to say, but I was thinking about you, and… well, I was thinking about how pretty you are. I was thinking about the sparkling shade of green your eyes are, and how pretty your hair looks in the sun…and how your cheeks turn pink when you are upset. Ever since we were young, I always can remember thinking you were a rare beauty."

Something unusual fluttered inside of Aimee when he spoke like that as he touched her so gently with the hand that was not busy restraining her. She had been told she was beautiful countless times by seas of men back in London, but never once had it quite affected her like this. She felt herself relax in his arms as the feeling settled in on her. All of those men had told her how pretty she was, but never once had a man who she thought hated her complimented her in that fashion.

But why was he complimenting her? Did he not hate her like she had always thought? She had probably known him since they were five years old or so, when he first came to their church. The memory of his first day at their congregation was still clear in her mind.

He had entered the sanctuary dressed in borrowed clothes that were a few years too big for him, and his eyes were red with dark circles underneath, no doubt from crying. His blond hair was tangled and longer than he wore it now, and he looked thin enough to be blown away by a strong wind. Reverend Dobbs had introduced him to the congregation as a distant relative who was now living as his son. The reverend had never married, so little Matthew had nobody to sit with during the church service. Aimee distinctly remembered how sad and lonely the little boy had looked in the church pew all alone. Aimee's parents had told her to stay away from him, because he was no doubt ill from being out in the streets his entire life. Aimee had seen him outside that day, surrounded by children who were laughing at him. Hating to see someone being ridiculed like that, Aimee had stepped in and scolded the children, holding his hand until her father came by and told her to never speak to the street rat again.

She had never known where Matthew had come from, just that their pastor had taken him in as his own son. When she had grown older and Emery had tried to speak to her after the church services, her maman had told her that he was not the type of man she should associate with, so it would be in her best interest to not speak with him. Besides, he was a pauper. She was a lady. They had no business together.

"So why do you hate me, Emery? Ever since I can remember, you have been aloof with me. What did I do to you to make you hate me?"

His hand stilled at the base of her neck. "Aimee, I don't hate you."

"Ever since we were little, since that first day when I defended you, you have avoided me at all costs. You acted like there was something wrong with me. And from the moment I stepped onboard your ship to help find Eden, you mocked me. Relentlessly. You called me *princess* and you ridiculed me when I was frightened of the rat, and…"

"Aimee, stop that."

"No, I will not stop. I think I should get a chance to speak, just as you did."

He looked upward with his midnight-blue eyes as if pleading toward Heaven for help. Thankfully, he did not try to interrupt her again.

"You have always acted like I am some spoiled brat whose company it pains you to keep. And then, you made me walk all the way across town with *bare feet* because my heel broke. And you—"

"And I waited too long to patch up the hole in your cabin that the rat had crawled in through. I made you move into my cabin with me, and then I spoke unfavorably about your favorite pink quilt."

Aimee only allowed him to interrupt her because he was speaking the truth, and because as he spoke, he loosened his hold on her ever so slowly, so she could move of her own will again.

"And I ordered you around. I told you that you should not speak to Mr. Honeysett. I asked you to stay away from someone you wanted to speak to, like I was able to tell you what you could and could not do. I thought bad thoughts of you." Would the man stop already? When he proclaimed all of the awful things he had done to her, it made her far less

72

upset with him. It made him sound a lot more human, and she did not like that when she wanted to be mad at him. She preferred to think of him as the irreversibly rude enemy, not the husband who understood the wrongs he had done her. "I spoke ill of you to your friends, like Eden and Ivy. I despaired at the thought of being married to you. I called you *princess* when I knew how much the name bothered you. I dragged you down to my cabin just a few minutes ago, when you did not want to come. I—"

Aimee needed to stop him, and she needed to stop him now, before he made her completely stop remembering his hatred for her. She could slap him in the face, but he would probably only catch her hand and pin her back against the wall again. No, she had a far better idea.

She freed her hands while his grip on her was loosened, and brought them up to his face to draw it close to hers. Because Emery was not an outstandingly tall man, she barely even had to stand on her tiptoes to reach his lips for a kiss. His blue eyes darkened before sliding closed. He tightened his arms around her waistline, and for once, Aimee believed they both enjoyed their shared kiss. Aimee rested her hands on his shoulders as his hands slid up and down on her waist. One of his hands got tangled up in her hair again, unraveling the last semblance of a braid that had restrained her curls. She felt her hair tumble out of her braid, finally loose.

Before they got too carried away, Aimee pressed one more kiss on his jawline and pulled back. Emery made a frustrated noise, still caught up in their embrace. Aimee had enjoyed enough kisses from former suitors to be able to tell that Emery had never kissed a girl before her on their wedding day. Well, now they had shared a grand total of three kisses, and she could tell that he was beginning to get the hang of it. She traced his jawline with her finger, before lowering it back down to his shoulder. Matthew Emery was a handsome man. That had been the first thing she noticed about him when they were teenagers and he had smiled at her shyly from the back of the church. Did he know how handsome he was? Probably not. Although he was always well groomed, he did not seem like the type of man to be concerned about his appearance.

"Matthew I think it is only fair that I tell you I have always found you handsome."

A smile graced his lips, a rare sight for Aimee. "You flatter me. No one has ever said something like that to me before. I have always been told I was short, and I wasn't worth anything because I was a filthy orphan. Your father told me one time that a man like me was not worthy to associate with you, his little princess. Apparently the situation my…my parents put me in was my own fault, and it made me like scum to people like your father and the rest of the society in London."

Her papa had said that to poor, young Matthew He had told that to Aimee all the time, in what she assumed was an effort to preserve her reputation so she could snag a wealthy, important husband. But he had said something like that to an innocent young man who had nothing but good intentions? Aimee's papa was a sweet man, and he always had her best interest at heart, but sometimes he took things a little too far. She was his youngest child, his only girl out of five children, and he tended to be a bit overprotective of her.

"Oh, Matthew, I am so, so sorry. I never knew that Papa said something like that to you." She pulled him closer for another embrace. "Is that why you have always hated me?" Realization hit her. "Why you have always called me *princess*?"

He leaned his head against her forehead. "I never hated you. But yes, I stayed away from you and tried not to befriend you after that. I didn't want to become attached to you when your father wanted me to stay away. I guess I came across as a trifle too mean toward you, though. It was not your fault that your father disliked me. But you were always distant to me, too. I used to like you, when we were children. I remember that first day, too, when you defended me. You held my hand and I almost cried. I thought you looked just like an angel with your golden-blond curls and your pretty, little, pink dresses in church every Sunday. It seemed like you had a different one every time I saw you, each more frilly than the last. I was enthralled by you, and your papa told me off when I got too close for his comfort. To be honest, you have always seemed like a princess to me. I never thought of it as a bad thing, until I used it that way and hurt your feelings. I think it means you are special, you are beautiful, and you are important."

Where was all of this coming from? Was he only being kind because he enjoyed their kiss and wanted more from her suddenly? Right now, though, Aimee did not care about the origin of their sudden amity. She was enjoying it too much. If they were friendly right now, maybe their marriage might not be forever doomed.

She reached up on her tiptoes to kiss him on the cheek before speaking. "I guess I don't mind being called princess then. So, Emery, you were going to answer my question a long time ago. What are we going to do at the islands we are sailing to?"

"Well, let me check how far away we are." He reluctantly released Aimee and strode over to his desk. Aimee felt cold in his absence. She could get used to having a man next to her all the time. Emery shuffled some papers around on his desk, and Aimee inhaled sharply. If he found the ink-stained papers that were her doing from yesterday, all of their amity from the past half hour would be completely undone, she knew it.

"No, don't worry about it." Aimee lurched forward and grabbed his wrist before he picked up the last paper that covered the ones ruined by ink.

"Why not?" He studied her closely, his eyes peering into her until she shifted her weigh uncomfortably.

"Because…well, because…" Aimee had a hard time to make an excuse. Why wouldn't he need to look at the papers? Well, she had learned one way to distract him recently. She reached up and kissed him.

Yet again, he responded favorably. His hands rested at his sides for a moment, as if he did not know what to do with them when he wasn't busy restraining her. Finally, he ran them over her shoulders, taking all of the tension out with his caring touch. His fingers wandered lower, down her back and to her waist. It was ironic, really, that they were enjoying each other's touch right now. Just the other day, Aimee had thrown up after their first kiss, and Matthew had not fared much better. Aimee could feel the muscles of his upper arms through his thin, perfectly pressed white shirt.

She had to make sure he was good and distracted before she let him go. Aimee knew a lot of ways to distract men who were falling for her from her days back in London, flirting with all of the eligible young men in the city. Her father had told her that the more men she got to adore her, the wider chances she had of an esteemed marriage.

Aimee pulled Mathew closer, until her curves pressed against him. He responded to that, moving his hands to her lower back and deepening their kiss. Emery had probably forgotten about his papers by now, but he was a stubborn man, so she continued as she was and lost herself in the kiss.

Emery broke their contact and pulled his head away. Aimee could not hide the hurt in her eyes as he nudged her a few inches away from him and pulled back his arms. A woman ought to be able to kiss her husband without him bristling about it. He seemed to sense her distress, and his hand reached out to cradle her cheek. "I do not know about you, but a man has to have a chance to breathe sometime, princess."

Aimee's insides softened at the sweet smile that warmed his handsome face.

"Now, Aimee, I have been trying to tell you of my plans for Hispaniola. Ever since Reverend Dobbs took me in off of the streets, I have wanted to become a missionary to serve God. Whenever I do some of my merchant work in the Caribbean or the Americas, I try to find some people I can share the gospel with while I'm there. I have also filled some vacancies in towns that need a preacher when I was near. This time, there is a village of native peoples in Hispaniola who have responded well to other missionaries, and want to hear more. They also could use some help, because some of them have fallen ill and need help with food and healing, things like that. I plan to help them out for a few days while I am waiting to pick up one of my client's orders of sugar cane."

Aimee had known Matthew traveled a lot and that he wanted to be a preacher one day, but she had not realized he spent his time helping the people as well. Did he want her to help him in Hispaniola? As his wife, she would be expected to do some work. Aimee loved to help other people, and had encouraged the ladies of her church to start a charity, but her parents had always taught her that it was a sign of low class to do such menial work. That was meant for servants. Between her parents, her brothers, her servants, and even her best friends, Aimee had barely lifted a finger for herself, much less for someone else, her entire life. She was excited at the prospect of actually getting to do something with her own hands.

Matthew chuckled. "I will not force you to do anything, princess, if that is what you are fretting about." He kissed her forehead as he walked around her. "Now. I have work to do, if you will allow me."

Chapter 6

Aimee would never get used to seeing so much lush greenery in one tiny location. Sure, England was also an island, but it was her home. The islands in the Caribbean felt almost mystic to her, unlike anything she had ever witnessed.

And they were crawling with insects.

A particularly large mosquito buzzed by her face before landing on her forearm. She managed to slap it away before it bit her. "Why won't these insects leave me alone?" She had not intended to shout, but realized her voice was a lot louder than it should have been. The men around her chuckled.

Matthew's hand steadied her waist as she trudged over a downed log. "Because, I suppose they think you are too sweet to resist, like most of the men you have run across. Except me." He chuckled and jumped back before she could hit him. His scent of cedar drifted over her, overpowering her sweet lavender. Maybe her problem was her favorite scent. Maybe mosquitos liked lavender as much as she did, but she could never give up the lovely flowery scent.

"You are an infuriating little man."

"Excuse me? I may be infuriating, but I am not little."

"Not little? You must be almost a foot shorter than Mr. Honeysett." She kept a light tone to her voice to assure Matthew that she was just teasing him.

Matthew stood up a little bit taller as he shouldered a branch out of her way. It was nice, really, that he was clearing a path for her in the jungle. Mr. Honeysett was at the back of the group, waiting for the others to clear the path for him before he ventured through the thicket. What did they expect from a man like him, though?

Matthew flicked a glance back at her. "There is a muddy spot here, princess. Watch your step."

Aimee stopped dead in her tracks, glaring at the puddle. Her pink dress was already torn and tattered from walking through this thick jungle, but she did not know what she would do with herself if it was coated in a layer of mud. Thankfully, Matthew seemed to recognize the panic in her eyes and took pity. He paused, grabbed her by the waist, and hefted her over the large mud puddle.

Before releasing his grip on her, his hands lingered on her and amusement lit his handsome face. His dark blue eyes brightened and a smile stretched across his lips. When he looked so handsome like that, all Aimee wanted to do was smack him in the face. Or kiss him. She was not sure which the most prevailing urge was these days, and that agitated her.

"What is so humorous to you, *dear*?" Aimee narrowed her eyes at him. What was he going to poke at her about this time? It was not her fault that she did not wish to further ruin an expensive dress by trudging through the mud like a workhorse.

Surely he understood it was not only a matter of vanity, but also money?

"You are lighter than a feather, even with all of those layers of skirts on you."

That was all? Aimee smiled softly and continued forward through the uncivilized island path.

Behind them, Mr. Honeysett faced the puddle with a running start and leapt over it. Matthew rolled his eyes and tugged Aimee along, nudging her in front of him, no doubt so he was between her and Mr. Honeysett's supposed treacherous intent.

"I wondered, Aimee *darling*—" Matthew emphasized the term of endearment as they now seemed accustomed to doing to one another, "—if you would be willing to help me perform some charity work in the camp when we arrive. I know I said you do not have to, and I will not force you to help. However, I think it would be wonderful for everyone involved, and we would be able to leave this island more quickly if you pitched in on the efforts. Besides, I think it would feel wonderful to have my wife by my side as I do the work I love to do. Will you join me, Aimee?"

Aimee had always been interested in aiding with charity work, but her well-intentioned father had told her that was the work of commoners. They were above work like that, he said, although they donated large sums of money to the church and several other charities.

Mr. Honeysett sidled up beside Aimee, placing a hand on her wrist. "Captain Emery, I do not understand how you could suggest such a thing of your dear, delicate wife." His rich, slightly accented voice slid over Aimee like sweet, sweet honey. She missed her mother's French accent. "Can you not see this

81

is a lady you are speaking about? She is not cut out to do menial labor as you are suggesting."

Aimee appreciated being spoken about as if she were someone treasured, but she did not quite like the belittling tone Honeysett adopted when he spoke about her abilities to help at the camp. She was not some fragile piece of china.

"Matthew I would be glad to help you in the village. I am sure I am capable of pitching in to help. I am not a child."

A smile brightened Matthew's face, and he grabbed her arm, gently tugging her away from Mr. Honeysett. However, Honeysett's grip on her wrist tightened, almost to a point that caused her pain. She gasped and squeezed her eyes shut. Although Aimee always seemed to find herself in some form of conflict or another, she despised it. And she did not want to be the subject of a game of tug of war between two silly men.

"You're hurting her." Matthew's eyes darkened and he immediately released her, taking a step closer to Mr. Honeysett. "Do not touch my wife."

"I am just protecting her from a man who wants her to overexert herself."

Aimee clenched her teeth as his grip tightened on her wrist, cutting off the blood from circulating to her fingers.

"Let go of my wife." Matthew uttered the words slowly, clearly. Menacingly. Aimee had never heard a tone like that from this man.

When Mr. Honeysett just sneered, Matthew shoved him away. The unexpected force sent Mr. Honeysett toddling backward, causing him to release Aimee. She turned to find Matthew waiting for her with open arms. For once in their lives, she had never been happier to fall into his embrace.

"You hurt my wife again, you are going to get a lot more than just a push, Honeysett."

Mr. Honeysett scoffed and raised his hands up in an innocent gesture. Matthew kept his arm about Aimee's waist as they continued their trek through the jungle. Sweat dripped off of Aimee's forehead, but Matthew assured her they were approaching their destination.

Sure enough, after a few moments, they met a clearing. As they neared it, Aimee noticed rows and rows of huts arranged in neat lines. Several native children ran about the rows, shouting and laughing. When they caught sight of their visitors, they stopped and rushed into several of the huts. After a moment, a tall man emerged from the hut, a smile on his face. Aimee expected him to speak his native language, but was surprised when he spoke near-perfect English.

"Welcome, Mr. Emery."

Matthew stepped forward to greet the man. "How are you today, chief?"

"We are trying to get along the best that we can, but we are lucky to have you here to help with us."

"We are glad we could come. I would like to introduce you to my wife, Aimee."

Another grin broke out on the chief's face. "A wife? Congratulations, Mr. Emery. She is beautiful."

Aimee felt her cheeks heat. "Thank you, sir. It's good to meet you. My husband often talks about his previous visits here, and how much he wants to return. I know he cares about the people a lot."

"Well, that's great to hear. We value our visits from him more than you can imagine." The man patted Matthew on the back heavily.

"Tell me, what is happening here? There is an illness

spreading?"

The chief's face darkened. "Yes, we are plagued by a sickness. Many of the children have succumbed to it, and the men and women are dropping now as well. I am afraid if we lose many more, our village will not be the same as it once was."

"Matthew, that is horrible." Aimee rested her hand on her husband's. Many illnesses had spread through London, some deadly, but she had never seen one in her life that threatened to wipe out their entire population. She could not imagine the terror the people were facing. It was an excellent idea to have Matthew there to help, especially with his goal to spread God's Word to the people. It seemed like they needed it more than ever.

"It is unfortunate, but we know that our lives will improve if you stay with us for a while." The chief gestured toward the village. "Now, if you please, I would like to show you and your wife to your place to stay, we have a small hut reserved for you—there should be enough space for the both of you—and we would be honored to have you join us for our meal tonight."

"Very well." Matthew nodded.

They were escorted to the other side of the village and shown a small, one-room hut. Aimee sighed. It wasn't like she was not used to sharing close quarters with Mathew already. It looked like they would have an interesting stay in this little village.

* * *

Chapter 6

Aimee was glad she knew a little French, even though it was out of practice. Most of the women on the island had learned some French from the settlers, missionaries, and colonizers that had passed through, so she was able to make some form of conversation with them.

The women lived in separate huts from the men for the most part, and the people did not wear much clothing. Aimee naturally wanted to be appalled at the scandal of seeing people in such a natural state, but Matthew had been quick to prepare her and explain to her that was just their normal way of living—as acceptable to them as her corset and layers of petticoats were to her.

Aimee smiled down at the girls who were crowded around her. She had not visited the ill yet—Matthew thought that it might be too much for her to be exposed to so much so soon—but she had started helping watch the children whose parents were ill or gone.

While she could barely communicate with the children, she found that they could connect with her over games she had played back home in London even if they did not use the same language.

"Mrs. Emery!" A little girl tugged on her skirt from behind her.

"What is it?"

The child offered her a flower. Aimee's heart warmed. "Thank you so much, little one."

Aimee never thought she would be doing something like this, but she was surprised at how much she enjoyed it.

* * *

Midday sunlight pierced Matthew's eyes and a droplet of sweat slid down his shirt. On a normal mission out here any other day, he would peel off his shirt and allow the sun to evaporate his sweat. But now, he was in front of a lady—well, his wife—and he did not wish to make her uncomfortable. He glanced over at her. She was doing much better in the weather than he had expected. Her cheeks were flushed with the heat, and her golden curls were weighed down with moisture. She huffed for breath, but not any more loudly than Matthew. She was one strong lady.

Thankfully, after a moment, they entered the jungle shade and were given a slight reprieve from the midday heat.

"How far away is this pond, Emery?" She hefted the large water vessel in her grip higher, shifting its weight. Matthew had given her the smaller vessel of the two, but he worried it would be too heavy for her once it was filled with water. They would have to take it easy on the trip back.

"Not much further, dear." Matthew shifted his grip on his water pot. She would be able to handle the journey.

Matthew could smell the water and hear it trickling amongst the other soothing sounds of the jungle. He already felt cooler in the late summer heat just thinking about it. A few more minutes of walking, and they finally arrived at the pond. It was really a river, dammed up to hold a reservoir of water for the people of the village.

"Oh, Emery, I don't believe I have ever been so joyful to see water in my entire life!" Aimee's bright tone lifted Matthew's spirits.

Matthew knelt down at the edge of the water and cupped it in his hands, drinking. Aimee remained a few steps back from him, still standing. He paused and motioned for her to join him. "Come on, dear, the water feels amazing in this heat."

Aimee crouched down next to him and peered at the water suspiciously. "I've never drunk water right from the ground like that. Is it safe?"

"It's all right, princess. Where do you think the water your servants fetch for you back home comes from?" Matthew offered his cupped hands up to her lips, and she accepted.

"It does feel good." She dipped her own hands in the water and patted her neck with the remaining cool droplets.

Matthew forced himself to bite back a mischievous grin at the idea that popped into his head. He could not allow her to suspect anything until…

"Hey!" Aimee sputtered as his handful of water splashed onto her dress. "What on earth do you think you are doing, Emery?"

Matthew flicked more water at the woman. After the last few days, she was in desperate need of some fun. They both were, in fact. Truthfully, Matthew had been in need of some fun for the past twenty-four years.

A slow smile spread across the woman's pretty face. Mischief flashed in her eyes. "Emery, *love*, won't you kiss me?"

Matthew had no idea what the woman had up her sleeve to attack him with, but another kiss sounded nice. It was worth the risk. He pulled the little, defiant woman into his arms and kissed her. They were getting better at that with each day of their marriage. Before they made contact, however, her hand was on his chest, pushing him backward with a surprising amount of force.

He swung his arms around for a minute to catch his balance, but that attempt failed. So, Matthew did what any logical man in his situation would do: grabbed onto his wife's waist and pulled her down with him into the water. The water broke his fall, and he broke Aimee's fall even further. Her eyes widened in surprise, and a little scream emerged from her mouth. Soft curves pressed against his body, awakening parts of Matthew that he knew were best to not think about.

The water was shallow enough that when Matthew sat up it barely went above his waist. Aimee tumbled out of his reach and also sat up. Her hair had fallen out of its fancy updo and now lay limp over her shoulders, soaked with the water. Her cheeks were flushed and her green eyes sparkled. Even her eyelashes were darkened, heavy with droplets of water. Her chest heaved up and down, up and down.

Suddenly, her face tightened, and she jolted upright, a horrified look crossing her expression. She bit her lip and shifted her gaze away.

"Aimee."

"What? Please, let me be. Let's get this water and return to the village, all right? We do not have time to behave like silly children." She splashed through the water to get back to the shore, but her layers of skirts were slowing her down.

Matthew rose and offered her assistance, but she jerked her arm away and shot him a glare.

"Aimee, dear, I hate to be presumptuous, but I got the impression from you that we were not going to fight each other anymore. What happened? Did I do something wrong?"

She finally stopped chewing on her lip, but then resorted to twisting her hands together over and over again, looking down. "No, I suppose you did not do anything."

"Then, pray tell me why you are upset, so I can make you happy once again."

"No, I will not tell you. I am ashamed and know you would

hate me for the reason if I told you."

"You are my wife, Aimee. I cannot hate you. I do not hate anyone."

She paused. Took in a breath. "Matthew, I am embarrassed because I look terrible doused in water like this. I was behaving like a child, and if my father only knew…"

"Aimee." Most of Matthew wanted to burst out in anger at her self-centered fears. But that was how he would have reacted a week ago. When he was not a married man. There was no way he would allow his temper and intolerance for women like his mother to rile his wife up. The other part of him wanted to tell her that she always looked beautiful, and she looked even more so right now. But there was no way he should admit to that.

"Shush, Matthew, I know I look terrible. My hair is all stringy, and my eyes probably look huge, and—"

"Aimee, it does not matter what you look like. Your appearance does not make you who you are." Matthew slid a slippery lock of hair back from her face and behind her ear. "Besides, I think you look beautiful, no matter if you just fell in a lake or not. Any sane man on earth could tell you that."

Her breathing halted, and she chewed on that lip again. "Thank you, Matthew. Many of my past suitors would never say something like that to me." A shadow seemed to pass over her face, and she looked down. "They only seemed interested in how pretty I was at the gathering we attended, or if I was wearing the most attention-getting gown. Now that I think about it, none of those men even knew me, and yet they proclaimed to be completely and madly in love. They…they all were interested solely in how I improved their status if they were courting me."

Matthew had to prevent himself from jumping in joy, grabbing this woman into his embrace, and kissing her. He had been trying all along to get her to realize that a person's appearances were not all that mattered in the world. All it took was getting her hair wet to make her realize that? They were surrounded by ocean, and had been for months. He could have brought that about a long time ago, if he had known.

"Come here, *darling*."

Her lips tipped upward in a smirk. Her hands rested on her hips defiantly. "Why, so you can pull me back down into the water and make me look even more foolish?"

"No. So I can do this." Matthew followed his urge to pull her into his arms. He held her there for a few moments, enjoying the feel of her in his arms. A woman he had never envisioned himself with, a woman who was now his. A woman he now cared for. It was mind-numbing.

"I suppose we should retrieve the water now, *dear*." Aimee pulled from his embrace, a blush staining her cheeks as she reverted back to their now familiar banter.

Matthew had never thought he would feel so strange without this pesky little woman in his arms.

* * *

Aimee tried to ring the water from her hair as Emery filled their buckets with fresh, cool water. The sun that filtered through the trees had already begun to dry her gown. Emery splashed water against his face and smoothed his hair back. It unsettled Aimee that, just a short time ago, this had been the man she despised most in the world. Now, she had no idea of her feelings for him. She suspected the sole reason she was warming up to him was because she was beginning to accept the fact that they were going to be stuck together for quite a while. And he had apologized. And...

"Are you ready?" Emery held out the full bucket for her.

"Oh." Aimee nearly fell backward with the weight of the bucket, but she somehow managed to remain upright. "This is heavier than I thought it would be."

"Is it too much for you? If you can't carry it, don't worry. I will make two trips. I don't care." A look of genuine concern crossed his face as he studied her, teetering with the bucket in her hands.

Aimee would be a fool to make the man venture out on the same trip twice because she was weak. But she was *not* the weak little thing that so many people back home, Matthew included, thought she was. "I can manage." She hefted the bucket up higher in her grip, sloshing water over the sides as she did so.

"Well, be careful. We can stop whenever you need to rest." He lifted his bucket in a manner so effortless it made Aimee angry. Why was this so difficult for her? It was just water.

Aimee took one step forward and nearly fell, due to her off-centered balance with the bucket of water in front of her. This was the heaviest object she had ever lifted. She had a manservant back home to take care of the men's work. Now she felt a little remorse about the amount of clothing she had packed into her valises for the men to carry. Next time she would be more kind. She took a few more steps forward, growing more stable with each step. It felt rewarding to do some work, actually.

They traveled in silence the majority of the way back.

Emery cast her a sideways glance as they neared the outskirts of the village. A grin turned up the corner of his lips. "I'm proud of you, Aimee."

Aimee halted, nearly dropping the bucket of water with the sudden loss of momentum.

"What is wrong? Do you need to rest?"

"No, everything is all right. We are almost there." Aimee was certain no one had ever told her they were proud of her before. She had been told she was pretty, or that she displayed perfect manners in a high social setting. She had been told she was the perfect asset to any man's arm. But never had anyone been *proud* of her. It felt...good.

Chapter 7

Aimee's spirits lifted even higher as she tended to a young girl inside one of the village's huts. She had been helping to care for the ill for over a week now, while Matthew did various work around the village. This shelter had been dedicated to the sick children, and several little ones and women rested on mats on the floor, all asleep except for Aimee's favorite. Celeste—or so Aimee had named her, because she didn't know the child's real name—smiled up at her and reached her hands out.

"You are a little sweetheart, aren't you?" The girl struggled to sit up, but her illness left her too weak. "It's all right, get some rest." Aimee patted the girl on the head, smiling at how smooth and soft her long black hair felt. Celeste strained to grab the ladle in Aimee's hand. "Oh, you're still hungry? That's good."

Aimee set her pot of broth on the floor and tipped a full ladle into the little girl's mouth. The girl spoke no language but her native tongue, which Aimee did not understand a single word of. Some of the natives also spoke French, but they were always busy with Captain Emery, who was teaching them lessons from the Bible to relay to the others in their own language. The chief was the only resident who spoke English.

That was no matter. Aimee and Celeste may not be able to speak to each other, but she found that she had no issues communicating with the sweet child. Matthew had told her that Celeste had lost both of her parents and all of her siblings to the sickness that was ravaging the village. The little one had a strong spirit, and Aimee believed that she would recover with time.

After Celeste had downed the broth, Aimee sat down next to her and pulled her into a hug. Celeste leaned her head back against Aimee's chest. "You are going to get better, *ma chérie*. I asked Captain Emery to pray for you specifically every day. I have been, also, but I thought it would be comforting to know that more than one person is praying for you, sweet one. He's a preacher, too, so that has to count for something, right?" The girl smiled up at Aimee with her large eyes—tinted with yellow from her fever—and tugged on one of Aimee's curls. Aimee hugged her even closer.

Although Aimee had done more physically demanding, exhausting work these last two days than she ever had before, bonding with this little girl had made her long days happy. She had not had much time to speak with Captain Emery, not that she cared too much. Mr. Honeysett, however, had made several appearances to her daily, each time encouraging her to sit down and rest. While Aimee appreciated the sentiment, she was no fragile flower; she was capable of helping others. "Thank you for brightening my day, Celeste. I have not had a very pleasant week, I am afraid. Well, that's selfish of me.

Look at you. You have been sick and you've lost your family. My apologies, sweetheart." Aimee pressed a kiss to the girl's forehead and whispered a prayer for her recovery.

"Aimee." She whipped her head around to see who disturbed her. Emery, of course. He was staring at her, something warm softening his gaze. From the looks of it, he had been there for a while.

"Yes?"

"It is time for dinner. I would like you to sit by my side tonight, to ensure that everyone realizes you are…taken. The men here are enchanted by you, and it makes me nervous."

Aimee restrained a groan. She did not feel like eating. She felt like staying with this sweet child for the rest of the evening. The poor little girl had not a soul in the world left to care for her. "I will join you in a moment. I want to stay with little Celeste for a few more moments."

A sad smile lifted the corners of his lips as he ambled over to her side and crouched down next to them. "She needs to get some sleep, Aimee. It will help her heal more quickly."

"I know that." Aimee was too exhausted to deal with this man. What business did Emery think he had, telling her what to do? She had spent much more time with the girl than he had. She knew what the little one needed. "Get some rest, Celeste darling." Aimee gently reclined the girl back on her pallet. The girl fought her, probably fearing that Aimee would soon leave her if she went to sleep. "It's all right, Celeste. I will stay right here until you fall asleep." She brushed smooth, shiny black hair out of the child's forehead.

"You're good with her."

Aimee had almost forgotten that the man was in the room as she had stared at the girl. "There's no need to wait for me,

Emery. I am going to stay here until she is sleeping. I can catch up with you to dine later."

"No. I am staying with you, wife, and I would like to escort you to dinner. Take your time with her."

Aimee settled down next to the young child and brushed some dark hair away from the little one's tan face. She began humming the melody of a French lullaby her mother used to sing to her in her cradle. The song always comforted her, and it brought a smile to Celeste's tortured little face.

Much to her surprise, Matthew chimed in, humming along with her.

After several minutes, Celeste was sound asleep and smiling contentedly.

Aimee turned around to find Matthew kneeling on the floor beside her, admiration warming his face. The man baffled her. She had not thought he would actually stay. Didn't he have other matters to attend to in the village? Either way, it was quite sweet of him to wait for her.

* * *

After dinner—which was pleasant despite the company of Mr. Honeysett—Matthew was enjoying a moonlit stroll around the village with Aimee. He did not recognize the woman next to him. He had been acquainted with her for years, and he had never thought this highly of her character. So, why now did she selflessly help these native women and children? She baffled him, but the changes warmed his heart. "Who are you, princess?"

A wrinkle creased her brow. "What do you mean, who am I?"

"Well, if I were a gambling man, I would bet that there were two different people trapped inside you." Her eyes narrowed as he spoke, and Matthew realized that what he was saying did not sound polite. It would be best to change the subject. "Never mind that, princess. I did not mean to insult you. I want to talk to you about that little one you have befriended."

"Celeste?"

She had named her? The sweet woman was far too attached to the ill child. "Yes, Celeste, if you call her that. I wanted to tell you how impressed I am at how well you have been taking care of everyone, and at how much that little girl looks up to you. I must say, I don't know many ladies from London who would go so far beneath their rank to take care of those beneath them."

"I'm simply helping you with your work. I have always been taught that in life, people are separated into stations for a reason. But since we came to this village, I saw that illness does not care who you are. The respected and the low-lives are all in those cabins together. So who am I to deny care to any of them just because of the family I was born into, or the family they were born into?" She crossed her arms across her chest, glaring up at him as if begging him to defy her. But there was no reason to be contrary.

"You are correct, and I am humbled at how far your beliefs have changed in the past weeks." Matthew grazed his hand against her elbow.

She blushed prettily. "I have been forced to change my ideas. I have a new husband whom I never saw myself being married to. Yet here I am."

Matthew inhaled deeply. Her sweet scent of lavender tickled his nose. Once again, he thought of her attachment to the little girl. He hated to darken her mood, but he did not want Aimee to be too disappointed later if something should happen to Celeste. "Aimee, sweetheart." For once he did not use the term of endearment ironically as he pulled her closer. "I have to advise you to not become too close to little Celeste."

She stiffened against his hold. "What do you mean, Matthew?"

"Aimee, you have to realize that the girl can't have long to live. I do not want you to get your hopes up about her."

The woman's bottom lip trembled. Her emerald eyes flashed fire. "Out of anyone, I would have thought that you would believe she could recover, *preacher*."

"I am not saying she will not survive, Aimee, only that 'twould require a miracle. She is too far into the stages of the fever. I just don't want you to be disappointed if something happens to her."

"I apologize, but I do not want to speak about this. I am going to retire to our cabin."

It baffled Matthew how one minute, they could get along like a house afire, and the next, like a happily married couple. Luckily, their evening walk had ended just in sight of the hut the good people of the village had allowed them to sleep in. Matthew waited to ensure the stubborn little woman made it safely into the hut, and then continued on his stroll. He would not go far, at least not away from the village, at night. He was confident in his abilities to defend himself, and he knew God was there to protect him, but he was not stupid. Wild animals were about this jungle after sundown.

However, Matthew desperately needed to clear his head. His wife was the most infuriating woman he had ever met. Matthew believed God had the power to heal Celeste and all of the people of the village. But he prayed that Aimee understood God would do what was ultimately best for those who love Him, and His answer to Aimee's prayers may not be the answer she wanted to hear. *Father, please help her understand.*

Matthew made his way to the center of the village. The moon was full tonight, illuminating his way. Lines of thatched-roof huts faced each other on either side of him. Everything here was so simplistic compared to the rich estates back in London. The Caribbean felt like a different world than the one he had lived in back home.

As soon as he saved up enough funds to support his missionary life—which he supposed would take longer now, as he would be supporting a wife, too—he would quit London and live away from it all. Aimee seemed to be taking kindly to life out here, at least as well as he could expect from her.

His walk had taken him to the edge of the village and the beginning of the jungle. He didn't know how long he had been out, but he supposed it was about time to return to his wife.

* * *

By the time Matthew returned to their cabin, he found his wife fast asleep. Moonlight poured through the window, illuminating her slumbering form. Golden curls tumbled over her chest, pooling onto the mat she slept on. Her skin had darkened a shade or two during her stay and the exposure to the sun. He thought the look became her. It made her hair seem all the brighter.

The natives had given them just one mat to sleep on, so Matthew had been forced to share it with his wife through the past week. Something not all that revolting anymore, honestly. But he did not wish to startle her while she was sleeping. What was he to do? Oh, well. He needed sleep.

Matthew pried his shirt off over his head, trying to disturb the woman the least he could. Normally, he would remain fully clothed around Aimee, but it was uncomfortably hot on this island. He folded the article and set it down on a wooden stool. Only then did he realize his wife was wearing less as well. Her frilly pink skirt was folded haphazardly and rested on the floor. Matthew shook his head and folded the fluffy thing neatly. Silly woman. He had begun to notice that, at least without her lady's maid, she tended to be quite messy.

He made his way over to the pallet where she slept. Would it disturb her when he settled down there? She might become frightened if she awoke. Matthew's cheeks heated. He had nearly forgotten that she had shed her skirt. All the lady wore was her chemise and stockings.

Matthew had never seen a lady like that, so he shut his eyes and lowered himself to the pallet next to her. If he did not see her, then maybe he would not feel the strange things he was feeling right now. Something soft and warm squished underneath his elbow. Aimee made a squeaking noise and tugged away.

Blast! He'd not only woken her, but he'd frightened her as well. "Shush, Aimee. It is all right. It is me. No need to fear."

She gasped and scrambled to prop herself up with her arms.

"You frightened me."

"I apologize. That was not my intention."

"That's all right. I am just...not accustomed to being awoken by a man touching me."

"That was purely unintentional, sweetheart. Go back to sleep."

That was easier said than done. He was far too close to the woman on their shared pallet, close enough that their shoulders brushed each time they inhaled. Her sweet scent of lavender teased his nose.

"Matthew?" She turned on her side to face him.

"What is it?" He propped his head up on his hand.

"How did you know that lullaby I was humming to Celeste this afternoon?" She fiddled with a loose thread on the sleeve of her chemise. "That was a French song my Maman taught me. I haven't heard it since I was a child."

Matthew's heart warmed at the memory of her soft voice comforting the child. "I...well, my mother had some...*friends*, shall I say, who were French when I was a little one. They would take care of me when she was busy, so I suppose I learned it from them."

"What was your mother like, Matthew? I never met her." He tried to not let her notice his change of breath at the subject of his mother. Everything in him wanted to object, to tell her to go to sleep and never ask him that again. But he supposed a marriage required honesty, and his wife deserved the truth. "Or do you not remember? You were young when you joined our church."

"No, I remember. It is difficult to talk about, but I probably should tell you about my upbringing."

Aimee's eyes darkened. She lowered her upper body back

101

onto the mat and rested her head on her arms.

He feared he had lost her attention already. "I never met my father. In fact, my mother probably only met him once. Although she thinks he may have been from Scotland. That's all I know."

That seemed to grab her attention. "What do you mean, Matthew?"

"My mother was a prostitute."

Aimee was silent for far too long. Shadows crossed her face, and Matthew wished it was full daylight so he could make out her reaction. Her lack of an answer felt like she had punched him in the gut.

"Aimee, the least you could do is say something. I did not condone my mother's choices, and I am not by any means proud of her."

"I'm so sorry." Her finger grazed his cheek.

"I don't need pity. I just thought you should know about my...unsavory past. My mother was an incredibly selfish woman, and my father was an unknown ruffian. I lived in a brothel, until my mother decided I was getting in the way and dropped me off on the doorsteps of a church without one backward glance. I'm not the rich, handsome suitor you were searching for. And although I have promised to be your husband, I would understand if you wanted to leave me after knowing what you are pledged to in marriage."

"Matthew, it could never be your fault! You had no choice in the matter. I would never hold something like that against you, something that you cannot control. You have convinced me that we are going to make this marriage work, and I don't want to stop our efforts simply because of who your parents were."

Her arm snaked around his neck, drawing him nearer. Her cute little nose was almost touching his.

Relief weakened every muscle in his body. "Thank God. Aimee, I was so worried you would hate me for this." He rested his forehead against hers as a smile formed on his face.

"Does anyone else know about your past?"

"I know it has spread around town back home. That's one reason I plan to be a missionary away from London—nobody wants a whore's son to preach the gospel to them."

"Oh, Matthew." Her breath blew out across his face as she sighed. "I can just imagine what they all say behind your back... do my parents and brothers know?"

Matthew would hate to discover their reaction to their daughter's sudden marriage. They may try to get an annulment, but as long as Aimee was not repulsed by his crude beginnings, he could not allow their separation. "From the way they have avoided me, I would assume so. I actually suspected they told you when we were younger, but I guess that wasn't something they wanted to discuss with their daughter."

"Matthew, I want you to know that I will not hold this against you. Believe it or not, I've grown to like you a lot in the last weeks. I don't want you to go anywhere." She snuggled closer against his chest, and Matthew marveled at the sensation of holding a woman that was his. All of this was so new to him.

"I like you too, Aimee. I'm glad that I was forced to give you a chance, because you are a good woman, and I have judged you most of our lives. I was so foolish." Having his pretty wife so close to him at nighttime was going to prove a temptation if they intended to keep their marriage in name only. He wished she would stop stroking her cheek against his chest. All he wanted was to kiss her, and they both needed to get some rest. So, he squeezed his wife and kissed her forehead instead. "Goodnight, *darling*. See you in the morning."

* * *

Eric Honeysett backed away from the hut's opening, only a touch of worry tightening his gut at what he had just witnessed. A small wrench had been thrown into his plans when he had learned that the couple actually did care about each other, but he was certain that their newfound trust in each other could be broken, and Aimee could be his with some work. The couple had shared a rocky beginning to their relationship, and Eric gathered it could still be shattered at any moment.

He didn't know why, but women were always a bit more enticing to him when it took a little work to get to them, anyway. And an enticing woman who came from a wealthy family? That was music to Eric's ears. If he could woo her into leaving her husband for him, he would easily be married to one of the wealthiest women he had ever met. If he got tired of her after a while, then fine. It would be time to move on to the next woman with a little money.

He chuckled as he walked away from the happy couple's hut, glad for the cover of night and the noise of the jungle. It would take a little effort, but it would be worth it to separate the little spitfire from her husband. Yes, Eric was due for some entertainment.

Chapter 8

When Aimee awoke the next day, Matthew was nowhere in sight. He had probably risen before her and was already at work by now. The man seemed to get up even before the sun every day, a custom that Aimee could never understand or embrace. She valued her sleep. The space on the mat next to her had already been chilled by the air, so he must have been gone for quite some time.

Shaking the thought aside, Aimee rose from her cocoon on the mat. She readied herself for the day, anxious to check on little Celeste as soon as she could. Aimee stepped out of the hut and was greeted by the smothering Caribbean humidity. A droplet of sweat already cut its path on her back, down between her shoulder blades. She should have used a little extra of her favorite lavender perfume to counteract the stench of sweat that was inevitable in this environment.

As she strolled down the path to the sick hut, a hand suddenly gripped her elbow. She collided with a hard body. Arms wrapped around her and pulled her back against the man tightly. A scream escaped her throat as fear ripped through her. She had been watching her path, and there had been no one in sight. Whoever this was had jumped out at her. They had been waiting for her. She jabbed an elbow into his stomach.

Just as she was about to scream for help, the man turned her around to face him. "Aimee, dearest. Hush. I saved you. See?" Eric Honeysett pointed to the ground in front of her. It was a large black snake, slithering along the path. Fear weakened Aimee, and she almost collapsed in his arms. "It looks like a young python. You need to be more careful where you are walking, my dear."

"A...a python?" Aimee had heard tales of the large, murderous snakes but had never seen one in real life. Panic ripped through her. Honeysett must have noticed her state, for he scooped her up in his arms.

"It's all right, mademoiselle. I have you. The snake is already gone. No need to worry your pretty little head." He touched his forehead against hers. Aimee thought his touch was a little forward, but she welcomed the human contact after that frightful encounter. She appreciated Matthew, but he would probably be laughing at her right now, just as he did when she was frightened by the rats. Honeysett, on the other hand, was here to comfort her for now. "Let's take you back to your hut, dear."

"I'm fine, Honeysett. It was just a scare. You can let me down." He seemed a little too comfortable holding her close, considering she was a married woman.

"No, you need to go rest after a scare like that. A fragile woman like you needs to be careful."

They were almost back to her hut already. "Mr. Honeysett, let me go. I am not a fragile woman. I can take care of myself. That snake startled me, but now I have to get back about my business. I am all right. No need to worry about me." Aimee swung her legs in an attempt to free herself.

"Fine, mademoiselle. Of course I will release you. I hope you understand that I was trying to see to your welfare."

"I appreciate the effort, sir, but I am not some fainting maiden in constant need of rescuing. Now, if you'll excuse me, I need to visit someone."

"Very well. I wish you a good day."

Aimee was surprised when the persistent man sauntered off, leaving her alone once again. Thank goodness. Now she could visit little Celeste. When she arrived at what had been designated as the sick section of the hut, she was greeted by several worried faces. One of the native women shook her head violently, motioning for her to leave and babbling something Aimee had no hope of understanding. In any other case, she would have run to find Honeysett to help her translate, but after how pushy he had been urging her to go rest, she was determined to figure this out on her own. The look on the woman's face warned her to leave, but she couldn't. She had to see Celeste.

Terror froze her for a moment. What was wrong? Was Celeste in trouble? "I'm sorry, ma'am, but I don't speak your language. I need to get in there. Please let me by. Maybe I can help." Aimee motioned toward the doorway of the hut. Finally, the woman stopped chattering and reluctantly allowed Aimee to pass through.

The sight before Aimee would forever be engrained in her mind. Little Celeste was being packed up in a bundle of blankets and carried away by a group of women. Matthew stood near them and was speaking over the limp body of the child, Bible in hand. "Wait!" Aimee screamed. She ran forward and placed a hand on Celeste's forehead. Cold. "No! No, she's fine. She's still here. She's all right. She's just asleep."

The native women frowned at her. Matthew tugged her away from the girl's body. "Aimee, she's gone."

"No! No, she's not gone. She was fine last night. She was here last night, I was with her and…and she's not gone!" Tears poured down Aimee's cheeks.

Matthew nodded at the native women before pulling Aimee to the side. "Sweetheart, I'm sorry. Aimee. Come here." He drew her into his chest and rubbed her back.

All Aimee wanted in the world was to be comforted by this man, but she could not allow it. It was not right to be comforted, when little Celeste had gone through so much pain with no comfort. The poor girl had died alone! Rage bubbled up inside of her. "You didn't tell me. Matthew, you knew and you didn't tell me. Maybe if I had known she was so close to the end, I could have visited her and comforted her. I would have run straight here. But she…she…*died* all alone here."

"Aimee, there's nothing you or I could have done about it. The women found her this morning. It happened during the night. She was already gone. I tried to warn you about how serious her condition was."

Aimee pulled away from her husband's embrace. "Please don't touch me."

Without his arms around her, she felt empty and cold, but she did not wish to be near him right now. She needed some time before she spoke to him again, or she might explode. "Thank you, Matthew, but you can go back to your funeral. I need some air."

* * *

Eric Honeysett found the lady sitting at the foot of a palm tree, her face in her hands, sobs racking her shoulders. Oh, this was too perfect for him to pass up. He knelt in front of her, certain he was maintaining the picture of a gentleman, and took her hand. Why was her husband not here to comfort her? Oh well, this was going to work to his benefit.

Her tear-soaked green eyes met his, and he almost felt genuine pity for her. What had brought her to this state of turmoil? "Oh, come here, sweet lady. Come here." He pulled her into his arms, unable to resist the attraction of comforting a distressed woman. She was shaking. Poor thing. Whatever had happened must have been far worse than the snake she had seen earlier in the day.

Much to his surprise, she melted into his embrace. Perhaps it would be easier to win her over than he had thought. He stroked her hair and breathed in her sweet lavender scent. She was an appealing woman, he would give her that. But all he was interested in was the money he could get from her family if he got Captain Emery out of the way and claimed her as his own.

Eric had been entangling himself with wealthy ladies of the Caribbean for years, quietly obtaining money through his involvements. One would be amazed at what a jealous husband would pay to leave an affair quiet. Aimee, however, was by far the wealthiest woman he had found thus far, and he could not wait to sink his teeth into some of her family's funds.

"Aimee, tell me what's wrong. Who hurt you?" He patted her back gently, wishing her tears would stop already. Females could be quite annoying with their emotional outbursts.

"Nobody...*hurt* me, Honeysett," she managed between sobs. He wished she would call him by his Christian name, as he had asked her to. His family name made him feel one more step away from her. "A little girl...*Celeste*...died, and I had grown to care very much for her."

They had not been on this island for long. How had the woman grown so attached to one of the ill children? She was probably overreacting, as women were prone to do. Oh well, he could not let her know he thought she was ridiculous. "I'm sorry, Aimee. I'm sorry." Yet again, she melted in his arms, and Eric marveled at his luck. She needed to be distracted, to forget about what had upset her. "Aimee, sweetheart, tell me about where you're from."

She sniffled. He pulled out his handkerchief, and she eagerly accepted it. "I...I hardly think now is the time to talk about my home, sir."

"You need to get your mind somewhere else, my dear. Far away from this island."

A frown creased her brow. "H-how about you tell me about your home then, Mr. Honeysett. I'm afraid I'm not good at conversing right now."

It unsettled him to talk about his past, but if it would distract the weepy lady and make her more inclined to trust him, then so be it. He did not have to tell her everything.

"Well, mademoiselle, my father was a Frenchman who owned a plantation here in the Caribbean." She did not need to know that his mother was a quarter-negro slave.

She rubbed her eyes. "And what about your mother?"

Of course the nosy little woman had to inquire about his mother. If he revealed his true parentage, she would not be interested in him. No woman ever was. "I never knew my mother well. I hardly ever saw her when I was young." She frowned, but did not pry any further. "My father died when I was about eighteen years old, and left the plantation to me. I wasn't interested in running it, so I sold it and live off of that hefty sum of money now. I am quite wealthy. I am working for Captain Emery because I have been craving adventure. I want to go out and see the world, not just stay at my plantation for the rest of my life."

Her eyes glittered as she looked up at him. His father had never had any other children, and after some paperwork forging, the plantation was his after his father had died. Eric may have already spent a large portion of his funds, but she did not need to know that. He needed to lure her into believing he was just as wealthy as she was or it would never work.

"My maman is from France, you know. Your accent reminds me of hers, but it's not as strong. You say some words the same way she does," Aimee said.

"Ah, I could tell you were as special woman, Aimee, and now I know why. You have French blood!"

That coaxed a soggy smile out of her. "I miss my home." Sadness crossed her face once more.

"When will you be home again?"

"Hopefully soon. Matthew seems to have a few more stops planned before we return to London, but I cannot wait to see my family and friends." She leaned her head against his shoulder, her breathing slowing to an even pace.

"I would love to see London. I have never left the Caribbean."

Her sparkling green eyes met his. Goodness, she was a pretty woman, and that just made him want her all the more. "You should come with us."

"I'm afraid your husband would not like that." Blast, why did he have to mention the man? He wanted her to forget about him, not worry about him. He was experienced in the art of wooing women like her, so slipping up like this was out of the ordinary for him.

"Matthew is just…protective of me at times. He would not deny you a trip to London if you requested it. I am certain." She smiled up at him trustingly then, almost making Eric cringe at the prospect of hurting her. Oh well, maybe the next time she was sobbing of a broken heart, her husband would learn his lesson and be there to comfort her.

* * *

Matthew had rushed outside immediately after speaking at the girl's makeshift funeral ceremony. It pained him to see the loss of one so young and sweet, but he knew God had taken her for a reason. He prayed the words he had spoken had gone beyond their language barrier and she had held a faith in God. Surely she was in Heaven right now. What pained Matthew the most, however, was his wife's agonizing reaction to the little girl's passing.

His blood ran cold when he found Aimee wrapped in the greedy embrace of Eric Honeysett. The cad. While every inch of Matthew longed to rip the two apart and pound Honeysett's face into the nearest tree, Matthew contained himself. Conflict would upset Aimee further, and she had already faced enough distress for the day. She likely only sought out the comfort that any pair of arms could provide, and was not thinking of how improper her embrace was as a married woman.

Her forehead was resting on Honeysett's shoulder, as he heard her suggest the cad come with them. The unfaithful minx! His mind warned him not to react, that it was just her state of grief acting, but his heart hurt. Images of his mother ran through his head, embracing a different man each night. Had he married the same kind of woman? Surely not. He bit his lower lip and stepped away carefully. Hearing any more would make him angry at his wife, and in her fragile state, she did not need his rising temper.

Matthew spun on his heel and sought the solace of the long stretch of beach on the end of the island. He loved his work here, but after nearly a fortnight and Aimee's traumatic experience today, something pulled him to move on. He said a silent prayer for the Lord to help Aimee through the mourning of the sweet child, and to help his marriage as he continued on his stroll. Tomorrow would be a long day as they said goodbye to their new friends and readied the ship for another adventure.

Chapter 9

Aimee hated the fact that young Celeste's life had been so unimportant to Matthew that he felt the need to pack up and leave the day after she had passed away. Goodness, did the man have no respect? She sighed rather obnoxiously and leaned her head back, trying to lose herself to the wind of the sea. Some salty mist hit her face, distracting her from her inner turmoil. She had let herself care far too much about Celeste; that was clear. But it was not her fault. Everyone who had loved that girl was gone. She had no one left in the world, and Aimee had been her only comfort. What else was Aimee supposed to do?

"How are you doing, mademoiselle?" Aimee startled. It seemed like Eric had popped up out of nowhere, but that was how he always seemed to appear.

Aimee tried her best to smile, but realized it was not convincing. "I will be fine, Eric. It was just…sad. I will be fine though."

He patted her arm. "I did think it was quite insensitive of

the captain to leave like that, right after it happened, don't you, mademoiselle?"

Aimee shrugged. She hated to speak poorly of her husband, but she had been thinking the same thing.

"There is no need for words, mademoiselle. I can tell exactly what you are thinking."

Aimee felt heat hit her cheeks strongly. It bothered her a bit that this man could see right through her.

"No need for you to be embarrassed. I just know you well." He smiled with that dashing grin that enchanted her. His aqua-green eyes were bluer in the sunlight. The tan of his skin made his teeth look even whiter, especially against the backdrop of his corkscrew black hair. He offered her his elbow. "May I take you on a stroll, mademoiselle? I know our quarters are confined, but I do think today is a lovely day for a stroll."

Aimee smiled and took his arm, glad for the change of subject from her husband and Celeste. The lack of deep conversation that Eric always offered was a pleasant reprieve. It reminded her of her days back at social gatherings in London. She was gifted in small talk. All of the men used to gather to speak with her, all meaningless, useless conversations.

Despite all of the recent trauma Aimee had faced, she allowed herself to revel in the shallow chatter Mr. Honeysett engaged her in for the remainder of the afternoon. For the day, it felt glorious to be almost back in London in her own way.

* * *

Twenty-four hours later, Mathew sat at his desk, glad that his wife was on the main deck so he was left alone with the cabin and his thoughts. Right now, they were docked in the nearest town, readying the *Cross's Victory* for another lengthy voyage. Although he had not revealed to Aimee about what he saw between her and Eric back on the island, he had not offered her as much compassion as he would have liked to offer. He was glad that he would have plenty of space away from her tonight when she took to sleeping on the cot and he would be back on the floor.

Never had the wooden planks seemed so inviting. He vowed to stay away from her for as long as he could while he waited for his anger to simmer down. He knew she had not intended to be unfaithful to him when he had caught her with Honeysett, but her actions had hurt him nonetheless.

A knock rattled him from his thoughts. *God, please do not let it be Aimee. I cannot see her without snapping at her in my anger, I am certain.* He opened the cabin door to discover a young lad of eight or ten years standing before him, his rusty orange curls shielding most of his freckle-dotted face. He had not been expecting any visitors at this port. How odd. Matthew rose sharply and approached the boy. "May I help you, child?"

"Mister, are you Captain Emery?"

"Yes, I am Captain Emery. May I help you?" Matthew leaned his head out the door and took in his surroundings, trying to determine if someone was with the boy.

"I have a letter to deliver for you, mister." With a flourish that befit a royal servant and contradicted his grubby attire, the child offered Matthew a folded up piece of paper.

Who on earth would write him a missive? Matthew had no family back home, and had no ties anywhere. How strange. Nonetheless, he accepted the letter from the boy and offered him a coin for his trouble. The lad's blue eyes lit up at the sight of the shiny piece, and he ran off in a burst of excitement.

Matthew sat down at his desk and tore open the letter, eager to discover what was important enough that someone had decided to write to him. It came from his colleague and confidant, whom he had met several years ago in London, and it did not look like good news. Reverend Melville had fallen ill, and his congregation in Charleston needed a reliable preacher. Melville remembered Matthew from his days in London and seemed to think he would be a perfect fit as a replacement for Melvile, at least until his health returned.

The letter fell from his hands, floating to the floor like a butterfly. Matthew? A real, sought-after preacher? Surely he was not good enough for the duty. He doubted he was even ready to be responsible for a small congregation. Nobody wanted him. But he re-read the letter three times and decided it must be truth. Matthew had just found himself his first real congregation, and it looked like Charleston would be their next stop before going back home. He hoped Aimee would grow accustomed to the stop-and-go life of being the wife of a preacher like him.

* * *

Several weeks sailed by uneventfully as they made the trip from Hispaniola to Charleston. Aimee loathed how the trust and understanding between her and Mathew had somehow seemed to disappear after they left the island. She had no idea what she had done to deserve this treatment. She had thought they had become close on the island, but after Celeste's death, he had all but cut her out of his life. No more hugs, no more smiles. He barely even spoke to her. She wanted to question him about his sudden change of temper, as she could not trace it back to anything she had done against him, but she feared she would revert back to her shrewish ways and cause another argument. Goodness, they had fought enough arguments to last a lifetime. Perhaps an absent relationship was better than a hostile relationship.

Aimee regretted her harsh behavior toward Matthew back on the day she had learned of Celeste's death, but surely he understood she had been in a raw emotional state. He clearly was not good at comforting a woman.

Eric, on the other hand, had been quite kind to her over the last few weeks. Their days had been filled with long—however shallow—chats and comfortable strolls along the deck. Why, this man felt more like a suitor than her own husband. He was seeking her, pursuing her. He actually seemed to care. If Matthew continued to mistreat her, Aimee might just allow her father to annul their marriage the moment she returned to London so she could marry a man who was *interested* in her, and Eric certainly showed an interest.

God, please let something change. Please let Matthew talk to me. I did not ask for him to begin with, so it would be nice if we could at least get along with each other. I did not choose to bring this upon myself.

A hand rested on her lower back. "All alone once again, my dear?"

"I am afraid so." She turned to find Eric comfortably close to her, a dashing smile plastered on his face. His nearness did not seem to unsettle her anymore.

"That husband of yours could do a better job of watching over you. Well, I am here now, so you are not alone any longer."

He leaned a little closer, his smile widening. "You look fetching today."

She felt her cheeks heat. Matthew had not complimented her like that in what felt like ages. It was nice to be near a man who appreciated her and took the time to let her know that he did. This was what she was used to, and she had missed it dearly. "Thank you, sir; you are too kind."

"Care to join me on a stroll, mademoiselle?" He offered her his elbow.

"Thank you." She took his extended arm and did not object when he pulled her closer to his side. Honestly, she did not mind if Matthew saw them and got angry with her. At least if she angered him, then he would say something and actually speak to her. His nonchalant silence was enough to drive her mad.

"I have something to speak to you about, mademoiselle." He patted her elbow as he pulled her another fraction closer to his side.

"Oh?" What could he wish to discuss with her? Usually their afternoon strolls were filled with nothing more meaningful than discussions about the weather or the latest fashions. Not that Aimee minded, however. She was quite popular back in London at all of the social events. Small talk brought her familiarity in the midst of all of the strange things happening around her.

Mr. Honeysett glanced around the main deck, which was mostly clear. The weather was good, so most of the sailors were free to lounge about until they needed more hands on deck. Mr. Honeysett leaned even closer to her, until his lips almost touched her ear. The warmth of his breath made the surrounding nerves tingle. His pleasant scent of citrus and wood drifted toward her nose. "I overheard something rather unfortunate today, mademoiselle."

"Oh?" She tugged on a loose strand of hair, preparing for the worst news.

"I overheard Mr. Emery speaking to some of his crewmembers. They were asking him about you, and he said something…well, something incredibly unkind." He leaned back, as if trying to gauge her reaction.

She tried her best to remain stoic, not wanting him to see her feelings. Who cared if Matthew spoke ill of her? It would not be the first time he had done so. She wasn't innocent, either. She used to spew insults about him all the time back home. However, Aimee had to take it in stride. She was not the one who had heard the comments, and she did not yet know what had been said. Mr. Honeysett could very well be blowing them out of proportion. "Please, Mr. Honeysett, do tell me what Matthew said."

"I heard him say he wished he had never married you. That his marriage to you was the worst mistake of his life, and he wished to get you off of his hands as soon as possible."

Aimee sucked in a breath. That sounded highly unlikely of Matthew. Had he not preached to her again and again that God had put them together for a reason and he would not be leaving her and she would not be leaving him?

However, Matthew had been acting quite strange in the last few weeks since they left the island, and she had not been able to discover why. Did he truly want to leave her? She had to admit the idea was painful to her. Was she that miserable to live with?

"W-when did he say that, Eric? Surely he was talking about something else." Eric was a bit of an odd man. Aimee would not be surprised if he was stretching the truth a little.

"It was yesterday. I was contemplating if I should tell you or not, but I thought it was in your best interest if you knew of his feelings. I could tell he has been treating you coldly since we were in Hispaniola. I have no idea what his reasoning is my dear, but some men are just fickle." He rested his other hand atop her elbow and brushed his thumb against her arm. "I'm sorry, mademoiselle. You deserve someone better than that scum. You really do."

Aimee jerked her arm away from his touch. "Please forgive me, Mr. Honeysett. I need to have a moment alone. I will see you tomorrow. Thank you for your warning about Matthew. I appreciate your concern." Aimee quickly found her way to the cabin and slammed the door shut, not caring if she had upset Mr. Honeysett by leaving him so suddenly. She needed time to herself. Time to pace, time to clear her head and *breathe* without being surrounded by men.

Should she address the subject to Matthew? Surely if she spoke of it to him, he would do something rash like forbid her from speaking to Eric again. As if he had the authority to push her around. No, it was better to leave the arguments and suffer in silence. She had learned her lesson.

A scuffling noise grabbed her attention from the other side of the cabin, startling Aimee. Of course, Matthew was in here. In her anger, she had not even noticed the wretched man's presence. Oh well, it served him right that she had ignored him as he had ignored her so many times in the past week.

Matthew was sorting through papers at his desk and seemed to be looking for something.

Oh no. If he kept up like that, surely he would discover the ink-splattered documents for which she was responsible. That could not end well. *Oh, please, Lord, not today.*

"Mrs. Emery?"

No. His voice was perfectly calm and even. Why on earth had he called her by their married name? That was such a silly, distant choice, and it probably meant he was furious with her.

"Yes?" Aimee faked a smile.

He held up some of the ruined papers, waving them in the air. "Do you happen to know what happened to my sermons?"

Guilt tugged at Aimee's conscience. She was almost tempted to lie, but knew she had to do the right thing. She had no idea that those papers had been sermons he had written, for goodness' sake. They were ruined beyond repair, completely unreadable, and it was all her fault. What a wonderful wife she had proven to be. Could she do anything right?

"Matthew, I am so sorry." Before she knew it, her chin wobbled uncontrollably and tears burst from her eyes, pouring down her cheeks.

He ran a hand through his hair before jumping up to pace about the tiny cabin. "Really, Aimee, must you cry when anything happens to you? That is such a silly way to deal with problems."

His comment made her want to cry all the more. There was no need for him to be cruel to her. She felt terrible about ruining his hard work.

"I am sorry. I tried to clean it up when the spill happened, and I did get some of it, but I...I didn't get everything. There was too much ink! I am so sorry, Matthew. Please do not be upset with me."

He inhaled deeply and stopped his pacing. "Don't worry about it, *sweetheart.*" He used the nickname in a mocking tone once again. "There is nothing that can be done about it now, is there? I will write some new sermons. They needed to be refreshed, anyway." He winked at her. Goodness, he had just switched his attitude within the span of a couple of sentences.

Aimee's tears slowed when she realized her husband was not furious with her. She longed to pry, to ask him why he had been so aloof with her lately, but she was certain the discussion would only trigger an argument. All Aimee wanted was some simple peace and quiet.

"I need some air." She picked up her skirts and ran out of the cabin at the highest speed her heeled boots would allow.

* * *

Matthew ran a hand through his hair, combing out a tangle as he did so. He needed to speak with his wife and resolve their unspoken argument before he blew up at her again over something as silly as ink-splattered papers. He was a foolish man. He was here to protect Aimee. In fact, he had vowed to love and cherish her.

So far in his marriage, Matthew was a failure, and he wanted to admit as much to his wife and beg for forgiveness. The next time she did something that troubled him, he vowed he would tell her that he was upset with her so they could speak about it. He could tell that his distant behavior had hurt her, and he wanted to make amends. No woman deserved to be treated like that.

How would she react if he tried to speak to her, though? She probably would not want to hear from him at the moment. He had hardly made a good impression the last time they had spoken, yelling at her for what must have been an accident. What a fool he was!

Matthew took a moment to freshen up and comb his hair before he went outside to find Aimee and make amends. It was time to act like a husband, something Matthew had been neglecting for several weeks now.

Chapter 10

Aimee held her skirt in one hand as she sped as far away from the cabin as she could. She was tired of this ship, sick and tired of the constant motion, the constant smells that assaulted her, and the way she felt confined in such a tight space with so many people she did not care to be around. The salty sea breeze toyed with her hair, tugging it out of her perfectly coiffed arrangement. The humid air seemed to suffocate her. She had always hated the outdoors.

Even though she fled to the opposite side of the vessel from her cabin, she still felt too close. The sailors on the main deck stopped what they were doing to stare at her, so she must look a fright. Weeks ago, they had seemed to grow used to her presence on the ship and they barely even noticed her. Aimee wiped tears from her face. She had almost forgotten that she was crying in her rush to get away from her cabin. So that was why they stared at her, then. She surely looked like a madwoman.

Aimee made her way back down the companionway, scurrying past the cabin she shared with Emery. Maybe if she went down into the belly of the ship, she could find some peace. She needed to get away from everything that reminded her of her idiot of a husband.

Foul scents of body odor and sewer assaulted Aimee's senses, but she hurried on. She had never been this far into the ship before. Normally, the darkness would have disturbed her, but it felt different today. The deep blackness seemed to comfort her, welcome her. A ladder that sat atop a dark pit seemed to beckon her down as she continued on her way. She felt tension sliding from her muscles. After a few moments, she stopped to appreciate the silence in the room. The rush of the water against the hull was louder here, but Aimee found it soothing.

She stood for several moments, breathing in the dank, damp air. After a while, a feeling of uneasiness crept over her. How would she see the way back to the main deck when everything was dark? She wasn't even sure where the ladder was even more. Oh, why was she always so foolish?

The air around her seemed to grow even warmer. If she didn't find her way in a moment, she would scream for help. Goodness, she would even accept Matthew's assistance right about now. She needed to get out of this veritable dungeon, immediately.

"If you are searching for something, mademoiselle, I might suggest using some light next time. 'Tis quite difficult to see in the dark."

Aimee shrieked and jumped as far away from the source of the sound as she could. Panic filled her, until she realized it was Eric's voice that had startled her. She could not see the man, but she knew she was safe now and he would help her find the way back to safety. "Oh, Eric." She reached her hand in the direction of his voice until it collided with something warm and hard.

Eric pulled her into his arms and rubbed his hand across her back. His hand lingered slightly longer than it should have, but Aimee suspected it was just him trying to find her in the darkness. "I've got you, mademoiselle. There's nothing to fear. What's wrong?" A scent of alcohol tainted the already rank air, and Aimee suspected it came from Eric. She had not thought of him as the drinking type.

She shook her head. "I'm silly, is all. I was frightened. I tend to get frightened for foolish reasons."

"It is dark down here, mademoiselle. I would understand if you were afraid. Let's get you back upstairs." He wrapped his arm around her waist and nudged her to the left. "Here we are. This is the ladder right here. Go on up." He braced his hands on her waist and boosted her up onto the third rung of the ladder.

"Thank you," she muttered as she climbed the ladder. The higher she climbed, the more light greeted her. By the time she reached the top of the ladder, her legs were shaking. She grinned at Eric when he joined her. "I've never been so happy to see light before."

He threw his head back in laughter. "Aimee, my dear, why don't you tell me what on earth you were doing down there?" Eric offered her his arm in a gentlemanly manner and led her up the companionway.

"How did you find me?" Aimee followed him as he led her past her current cabin, to the cabin she had shared with Ivy before she had become a married woman.

Eric knocked, but when there was no answer he opened the door and insisted she enter before he followed her inside. "I saw you running on the deck earlier. You seemed distressed, so I followed you."

"Why didn't you say something sooner? I was terrified down there." Aimee pouted as she sat on what once was her cot.

Eric turned as if he were to leave, but she touched his sleeve. "Please, stay, Mr. Honeysett. I want to speak with you."

"Very well. I wanted to see what you were doing, mademoiselle. I assumed you had gone there with a purpose." He sat down next to her, just a little too close for propriety. Aimee didn't have the energy to insist he sit further away, though. Besides, there was no sufficient seating arrangement in this room. Propriety flew off the deck the second you stepped foot on a ship, Aimee supposed. His breath was definitely tainted by rum, or something of the like. "So, what were you doing in the hold? What had you so distressed?"

Normally, Aimee just spoke small talk with Honeysett. But she had grown more comfortable around him, so she supposed it would not hurt to be honest with him. He seemed to have her best interest at heart, and he had saved her from the darkness of the hold. "I needed some time away from everything. I'm afraid Matthew is upset with me, and if he isn't, then he has every right to be. I am so foolish to think that things were working in our marriage when they aren't. I am a failure at being a wife and even being a friend."

"Oh, Aimee." He pulled her closer, so her forehead rested against his shoulder. Since when had this become normal for them? Oh well, he was simply comforting her as a friend. "You are not a failure at anything. You are the most fascinating woman I have ever met. I am honored to know you."

"Do you really think so?"

"Of course. I think you're beautiful. Your hair is so soft, and it looks like spun gold." His fingers caressed the hair near her cheek. "Your cheeks are always a pretty pink. Your eyes are like the rarest sparkling emerald. And your lips." His gaze lowered to her lips, and Aimee's heart fluttered. She longed to say something to him, to tell him he was speaking improperly to her, that he was touching her improperly, a married woman, but her breath was lodged in her throat. "Your lips are just so…" His thumb stroked her lips.

Aimee leaned away from his touch just enough to avoid it but not offend him. What was she to do? She knew it was wrong of Eric to be flirting with her so. The door to the cabin should be open for propriety's sake. This reminded her of a time at a ball in London. A handsome man—who she was certain she could snag in marriage—had led her away from the noise of the crowd and into the private study. The man had kissed her and wanted more under the influence of spirits, and Aimee had allowed his advances at the time, hoping he would propose to her. However, Aimee finally had the good sense to stop him and leave the room before things went too far.

But Eric was so handsome, so persuasive, so full of empty compliments…it was difficult to say no. And with her husband's aloof behavior, it would not be wise to burn bridges with a wealthy man who would gladly marry her should Matthew decide he did not want her any more.

Eric studied her before cupping a hand behind her head. He drew her closer, suddenly, his lips were pressed against hers. He tasted like rum. Everything in Aimee's body screamed for her to stop, to push him away, but she worried about what would happen if she did. Tears pooled in her eyes.

A stone seemed to sink in her stomach. She moaned, not out

of pleasure, but out of the terrible feelings coursing through her as she tried to pull away. Memories of Matthew's kiss crossed her mind. When Matthew had been kind to her, she had eagerly awaited his generous kisses. Right now, she longed for Matthew or anything that could get her away from Eric. She needed to pull away.

Eric seemed to mistake her moan for one of pleasure, for he deepened his kiss as his hands roamed over her body. She tried to pull away, but he held her tight, oblivious. Ever so slowly, he nudged her until her back was flat against the cot and he was on top of her. This was too far. Any girl with any sense knew that, but how was she to stop him?

His hand wandered to the back of her dress. After a few seconds of struggling, he fumbled with the clasp at her back.

That was enough. Her hand made it to her shoulder and she shoved him backward, her nails digging into his flesh.

"No, please, Eric." Her voice was muffled, but she knew he could understand her.

He ignored her, not stopping until her shoulders were exposed.

Goodness, what if she was not able to stop him? Panic seized through her body. Her limbs felt like they had turned to jelly. This was so out of the normal for him, a gentleman. The alcohol he had imbibed in must be clouding his judgement. "Eric."

It was a struggle just to breathe with the way his lips were against hers relentlessly.

Suddenly, Eric was gone. Air rushed to Aimee and she gasped like a drowning person, gulping in the sweet oxygen.

"What do you think you were *doing*, man?" A voice clanged against the close walls of the cabin. It was Matthew's voice, but it was as if Aimee had never heard it before. It was laced with utter rage and contempt. Aimee shivered and prayed none of his anger was directed at her. She scrambled to the end of the cot, as far away from the men as she could.

Eric responded to Matthew's fury with a cocky grin. He pushed against Matthew's shoulders with both of his hands, defiantly maintaining eye contact. "Mayhap you should ask the lady what was going on. She was enjoying every second of my attentions. Weren't you, *mon cherie?*"

Aimee wished she could sink back into the cot and disappear forever, but because that was impossible, she did the nearest thing and tugged her dress up on her shoulders for decency's sake. She feared Eric had torn the fabric in his efforts to undo it. A shiver ran down her back. How close had Eric come to…compromising her? The thought was unnerving. Why, the only time she had been happier to see Matthew was a month ago, when he had saved her from the auction in Port Royal.

Finally, Matthew seemed to notice her. His eyes dropped down to the condition of her gown. Goodness, she hoped she would be able to mend it. Only a handful of gowns had been able to fit in her trunks on the journey, and she had already over worn all of them. One was already ruined from her stay on the island.

Matthew growled and grabbed the man by the collar of his shirt. "Did you hurt her?"

* * *

Fury caught fire in Matthew until every inch of him was aflame like he had never felt before. This man had been kissing his wife. Not only kissing her, but he had been all over her. On top of her. And egad, the state of her dress! What an uncivilized scoundrel this man was.

And then there was his stupid face. He looked so pleased with himself to have bested Matthew and stolen the affections of his wife. Oh, fire and fife. What if he had not been harming Aimee? There may have been no struggle. She may have been enjoying her time.

The thought infuriated Matthew even further.

"Your wife is quite pleasing, sir. I am surprised you do not entertain her more often. I do not think you know what you are missing."

Matthew did not even know he had hit him until his fist stung and the man's face had bucked to the side. He could not help but feel satisfaction when Honeysett groaned and rubbed his jaw.

"Scads, man. If I had known you actually cared about her..."

Before Matthew could stop himself, he had swung a blow right into Honeysett's nose. "My wife and I are none of your business." He clunked the man back against the bulkhead for good measure. What would make this man learn? Matthew did not want to lock him in the hold—what if Aimee would resent Matthew for it? "Now get out of here before I have the sense to put you in the brig."

Honeysett sneered as he sauntered past Matthew on his way to exit. "Good day, Captain."

As soon as the blasted man left, Matthew turned to Aimee. She sat perched atop the cot, her arms wrapped around herself. This was not unlike to the last time Matthew had seen her in here. She had been shrieking in here with her friend Ivy, frightened to death by a small mouse. Now, that fright had come from a much more sinister cause.

"Aimee." He rushed to kneel at her feet. "Did the blasted devil hurt you?" He grasped her hand and looked at her partially exposed shoulders, which were marked red from Honeysett's touch.

"Oh, stop fretting over me already." Her eyes flashed fire and she drew her hand away.

"Goodness, Aimee, I would think that you would be more kind to the man who had just saved you." He studied her carefully. Her expression remained stoic. Perhaps she was still angry at him. Or... "What, was Honeysett telling the truth? Were you enjoying his affections?"

Her pretty face scrunched up tightly. Matthew did not know what that meant, but her lack of a reply was almost as good as an answer. What a fool he was, thinking she would remain faithful to their marriage. He had seen her in London. Every week, she was on the arm of a different suitor. A woman like her did not stay tethered down to one man. Of course she could not resist kissing the first man who showed her affection, especially when her own husband lacked in doting on her. Matthew knew women just like her.

His mother was one of them.

Matthew gripped her wrist and tugged her to stand. "Come on now. We are going back to our cabin."

"Why must you be so demanding?" She snapped as she followed him up the companionway to the captain's cabin.

Well, at least he had gotten some words out of her. She had barely spoken since he had found her in Honeysett's embrace. Matthew knew his best approach was to reign in his fury. He did not know her side of the story yet, because she had not told him.

He gave her a not-so-gentle nudge into their cabin and slammed the door shut. "Care to tell me what happened, *wife?*"

She crossed her arms defiantly. "What is the use? You would not believe me anyway. You are a brute, just like him."

He sighed. "I would venture to guess that you have kissed this man more than the two times I have found you in his embrace." That only made sense. She had probably been having an affair right underneath Matthew's nose all along. No wonder she always seemed so eager to get an annulment. What a fool he was.

"No *he* has only kissed *me* twice. And the first time was an accident."

Oh, certainly. I always go around kissing ladies involuntarily. Matthew kept the scoffing to himself, though, for he still wanted to hear what his wife had to say. He hoped she could alleviate his fears. "What about this time?"

She looked down and fiddled with her gown. "I will admit I did not push him away from me immediately, but he barely gave me a chance to speak. I was afraid. I did not know what to do."

Matthew's blood heated. He did not want to hear this, but he forced himself to listen.

"I did not stop him because I wanted him to like me. I knew if I told him to stop, he would become angry, and…and he would stop talking to me. Just as you stopped speaking to me." Her bottom lip trembled, and Matthew could not be certain if this was one of her feminine ploys or if she was truly upset. Egad, was she going to blame this on him? It was her fault to begin with that he had ignored her. "He kissed me at first, and I did not stop him. But then, he would not let me go. He kept kissing me, and then he had me pushed back against the cot, and…he started to undo my dress and he was touching me." Tears burst from her eyes and she frantically tried to wipe them away with the back of her hands.

"Come here, sweetheart." Matthew could not quell the urge to pull her into his arms and dry her tears. He trusted her. Believe it or not, he felt no doubt. She was telling the truth. "But why, Aimee? Why should you care what he thought of you? You're married to me."

She buried her head against his chest as her sob rent the air. "You have ignored me ever since we left the island. I assumed you were tired of me. Most of my suitors back home got that way. They acted like I was their whole world until they got some kisses from me. Eventually they moved on to the next woman, and left me to the next man." Egad, that was why she had moved from suitor to suitor? Matthew had assumed *she* was the flighty one. "I knew that if you were tired of me and had given up on our marriage, I should move on to Eric. He comes from wealth."

A growl escaped his throat. "Aimee, what were you thinking?" He pushed her away from him just far enough to give her a good shake. "I am not one of those men from London. I would never do something so stupid to you. I would never break my vow. I could never cast you aside. How could you think something like that of me?"

"You gave me no other evidence to follow!" She tried to shove against him, but he held her steady.

"What about Port Royal? I could have left you there alone, you know. You got yourself into that mess, not me. Do you *know* what they were going to do to you there?" He gripped her upper arms.

"Well, I certainly got an idea." Her sassy mouth would have gotten her into even deeper trouble with those men.

There was no polite way to put it anymore. Maybe shock would sink some sense into her pretty little head. "You were going to be ravished, Aimee. And then sold every single night as their prostitute. Do you understand?"

"Yes, I understand! Maybe I would have been better off there alone. Maybe I could have taken care of myself." She wrenched her arms from his grip.

Did she jest, or did she truly hate him so much? "Aimee, I fear you forget. My mother had that fate. I was too young then to understand what she went through every night, but now I do. A different man in her room, sometimes multiple each evening, using her and mistreating her. I would not wish that life on anyone, let alone the fragile society flower you are. I had to protect you, and honestly, I would do it again in a heartbeat."

"I am not some fragile flower! I can take care of myself, with or without you."

"Aimee, *love*, obviously you were unable to take care of yourself when I found you in Port Royal. You had no way out of there."

Her face grew red. She had to realize she was not going to win this argument, and yet she sat there sputtering.

He did not argue with her to make her feel bad. Matthew simply wanted her to realize how her choices could lead her to a miserable life. She needed to know he never intended to hurt her feelings. With a quick tug, Matthew had her back in his embrace. "Aimee—"

"No!" She jerked away from him so violently she nearly toppled over. Mathew reached out to steady her, but she snapped her arms from him. "When will you men understand the word no?"

Matthew almost bent over from the force of her words. How ignorant he had been. Well, he had gotten what he deserved. Now, she was categorizing him with Honeysett and all of the ridiculous, lusting, self-centered men she had courted in London. "Oh, sweetheart, I never—"

Aimee dismissed him with a wave of her hand and sped out the door. Now was not the time to pursue her.

Once Aimee was out of sight, Matthew threw his head back, closed his eyes, and prayed for wisdom on how to comfort his wife when she would let him speak to her. He had judged her for so many years, never realizing how the men she seemed attracted to always hurt her, using her only to their advantage. Although Matthew had never been invited to one of the parties Aimee had frequented, he could now imagine her speaking to the men, no doubt deliberately making herself sound more simple-minded than she was, just to win the heart of a controlling man. She probably went home and sobbed every week when the men moved on from her and she went on to the next. It pained him to know he had not been there to comfort her.

Egad, when had he begun to feel this way about Aimee? When had he started to care about her with a care deeper than the promise he had made at their marriage? The very thought scared him, and he feared they both needed some space before he could know what he was feeling.

Chapter 11

Aimee leaned against the main deck's railing and willed her tears to stay where they were. She hated how she had snapped at her husband. She *should* have been happy when he had saved her from Eric in his drunken state. But Matthew never failed to say something that upset her, and then they always argued. *Lord, please help me. Please give us peace. I want to get along with him.*

The ocean breeze did little to calm her nerves. Her hair tangled around her neck, and she made no effort to put it back in its place. There were no men she wished to impress onboard this ship anymore. A shiver crawled down her neck, and she scanned the deck for any signs of Eric. He must have crept back down to his cabin, so she was safe for the moment to close her eyes and breathe in the fresh, crisp air. Thank goodness they were almost to the Province of Carolina. Maybe once she was not confined in close quarters with her husband, she would find him less infuriating.

"Captain! Sails were spotted."

Oh, great. Now his stupid sailors have to summon him up onto the deck with her. Just what she needed.

Matthew arrived on the main deck, glanced at her, and then moved toward his men. He snatched an eyeglass from one of the men and looked through it for a moment. "It's the *Siren's Call.*"

Aimee's breath snagged in her throat. Her friend Ivy had been aboard that ship last she had seen her, sailing back toward London with a handsome pirate. What on earth was it doing back in Charleston?

"Matthew!" She called across the ship, not about to move closer to the infuriating man. When she caught his attention, she shouted, "Is it Ivy?"

He strolled closer. "Perhaps. I know that is the ship she left on. Did you think I would let our friend get on board a ship with a man I have never met and not remember the name of the ship?"

Aimee shot a defiant glare in his direction before skirting around him and to the other side of the ship. In Aimee's mind, they could not reach Ivy soon enough. She needed her friend and she needed her *now.*

All of the events of the past month rushed back to her. Her moments spent almost being sold in front of those terrible men in Port Royal. Matthew—the one man she had always hated—being stupid and saving her. All of their arguments, up until their fight today. She was about ready to punch him in the face—if a lady were to punch a man in the face—by the time their ships were lashed together by the men.

The second they were close enough to the other ship, Aimee braced herself on the bulwarks and launched herself over to the other side. It took quite an effort, considering all of her skirts, but she landed on her feet, which she thought was something to be proud of.

Every muscle in her body longed to run to her childhood friend, Ivy, and beg her to make everything in her life right again as she often had with Eden and Aimee back in London. Her friends were always there, looking after her and making everything right. But Aimee knew she was no longer a young girl who could cry to her friends the moment something went wrong. So, she simply glared at Matthew back on the *Cross's Victory* for a moment before speeding toward her friend.

"Aimee, what's wrong?" Ivy took a step closer to Aimee, and only then did Aimee truly look at her friend. She looked so different that Aimee almost backed away from the unfamiliarity. Ivy's face was bright, almost radiant. Her hair was much looser around her face than normal, and her eyes sparkled. But the biggest difference of all was the small, red-headed child she held in her arms and the hand that Captain Thompson had rested on her waist. "Aimee?"

Oh, yes. She asked a question. Aimee struggled to move her mind from the changes before her. "Ivy, I would like to introduce you to my *husband*." Aimee gestured across the ship to Matthew, who appeared just as shocked as she was to find Ivy with a child and so close to a man.

Ivy sputtered a bit and leaned back against Captain Thompson. "Aimee, you are jesting."

"Nay." Matthew had followed Aimee onto the *Siren's Call* and now wrapped an arm around her waist. She resisted the urge to jab an elbow into his ribs as she forced her brightest smile for her friend.

"She is my wife now," Matthew said

Aimee fought the desire to roll her eyes. She could tell from the tone of his voice that he was not happy either, so why was he trying to pretend he did not hate her with every bone in his body?

"Aimee, I am so sorry." Ivy seemed genuinely heartbroken.

Aimee was positive from the ripples through Matthew's body that he was chuckling to himself. She bumped her elbow into his ribs, just enough to warn him that she was unhappy but not enough to hurt him too seriously. The breath whooshed out of him, and satisfaction warmed her blood. He winced and rubbed his side with his other hand. Good. He deserved it. Their situation was not humorous in the least.

"Ivy, you must tell me what is going on. Who is this little one?" Aimee smiled at the little girl tugging on Ivy's hair.

Ivy's face brightened as she handed the girl off to Captain Thompson. "Are you and Captain Emery in a rush, or do you have a couple of hours to talk with us?"

Aimee looked to Matthew, who spoke, "I have to be in Charleston on some business before night falls, but we will always have some time for our friends."

"Oh good!" Ivy clung to Captain Thompson's arm.

"Please, join us in our cabin. Would you like some tea?" Before they could respond, however, Captain Thompson was already commanding one of his men to prepare some tea for them.

Matthew placed a hand on the small of Aimee's back and nudged her forward. She was so numb from shock that it was difficult to get her legs moving. Had Ivy said, "our cabin"? Had Ivy married Captain Thompson? One of their last conversations flashed back in Aimee's mind.

"I will miss you so much." A sob had choked her voice. "Please don't run off with some pirate like Eden did. What will I do all by

myself?"

Ivy had chuckled, pulling Aimee into a hug. "It will be all right, Aimee. I'm not going to get married to some uncivilized pirate. I am sure Eden has good reasons and knows what she is doing, but I would never do something like that. You have nothing to fear. I will be waiting for you when you return to London, and all will be well."

Well. It appeared as though Ivy had been wrong. She seemed quite attached to this pirate captain and the child they took turns holding. Was it the destiny of Aimee and all of her friends to end up wed to a stupid sea-faring man?

Captain Thompson held the door open for everyone as they passed through. Matthew pulled out a chair at the captain's small table for Aimee, and sat down after she was seated. Ivy sat across from Aimee, with Captain Thompson close to her left.

A few moments of rather awkward silence passed, as they looked back and forth to each other.

"So who should speak first? I am afraid all of us have a lot of catching up to do." Aimee wrung her hands together in her lap, anxious about all of the change she and her friends were experiencing. Goodness, this never would have happened if they had all stayed at home, happy in London. However, she had never experienced as much adventure as she had in the last few weeks, so she supposed she appreciated the reprieve from the stuffy boredom of her life. What had her friend's life been like in the last month? "Please, Ivy, tell us what's going on. I cannot wait a moment longer."

"Well—" she began, pausing as Captain Thompson entangled his fingers in hers, "—as you know, I boarded Gage's ship with the intention of getting to London more quickly."

Matthew chuckled, his laugh a low rumble. "Lady Shaw, my dear, I'm afraid none of us have made it to London."

Ivy smiled. "You're right; God must have had other plans for all of us. Gage and I made it through many obstacles to get to Charleston, where his sister was living as a recent widow. We came here to save her."

"Ivy, I believe that you are neglecting to tell us an important part of your narrative." Aimee gestured to Captain Thompson, who was still holding Ivy's hand and cradling the child in his other arm.

Captain Thompson used the opportunity to speak up. "Ivy and I found little Emma abandoned on the front steps of a church. We took her in and love her as if she were our own."

"The both of you?" Matthew pried. Goodness, getting information from these two was a struggle.

Ivy smiled shyly. "Gage and I were just married. In fact, you just missed seeing Eden and Caspian."

Aimee wanted to congratulate her friend, but the shock of this news was too much. It seemed as if *everyone* was married these days. And she had not even waited for Aimee!

"Aimee, you must tell me what has happened. How is Matthew your husband?"

Matthew grabbed Aimee's hand in his, and her breath stopped in her throat. The way he rubbed his thumb against the top of her hand sent pleasant shivers through her. It was unsettling, really. Especially when she intended to be angry with him. He needed to stop distracting her from that. "I found Aimee in a disreputable tavern in Port Royal."

Ivy gasped.

Aimee squeezed his hand, digging her nails into his palm as hard as she could. "That is not the way you should word it,

Matthew."

"I apologize. My wife is correct. She had been pulled off the street by some men, and they were…attempting to sell her in their tavern. I attempted to save her by telling them I was her fiancé, but they said they would only believe me and let her go if I married her right then and there. So, here we are now."

Ivy cast her a pitiful glance. "Aimee, just say the word and I can go speak to you about this…privately. Surely there is something we can do if you are unhappy in this."

Aimee resisted the urge to roll her eyes. She had already tried everything to pretend this had never happened. "In truth, Ivy, it is not all that bad." In the midst of their many arguments, there had been bright moments. The time he had defended her against Honeysett, even when she didn't deserve it…the kisses she and Matthew had shared and the quiet conversations… the teasing way they addressed each other. The bad might outweigh the good right now, but in reality, no matter how much her pride got in their way, this marriage was a far better fate than what would have befallen her in Port Royal.

Matthew's hand squeezed around hers more tightly. She glanced at him and noticed that his eyes were wide, and a cautious smile turned up the corners of his mouth. He seemed to be trying to thank her with his eyes, and the thought warmed Aimee's insides.

"Aimee and I are adjusting to married life, Lady Shaw, but I appreciate your concern," Matthew said.

Chapter 12

Matthew braced his arm around his wife's waist as they waved goodbye to their friend. For some reason, when he was around Lady Shaw and her new husband, he felt the need to stake a claim on Aimee. And for whatever reason, Aimee did not fight him off as much when she was around them either.

"Did you mean what you said to Lady Shaw, Aimee?"

"You mean what I said to Mrs. Thompson?" She spoke without looking at him.

"Yes, I suppose." Her forehead leaned against his shoulder. He held her close with one hand and brushed the hair away from her neck with his other. "So did you mean what you said to Mrs. Thompson?"

"About what?" she said breathily, he hoped because of his touch.

"That life is not so bad being married to your worst enemy?"

He felt her chuckle, more than he saw it. She buried her head closer to him. "Of course I meant it. That does not mean

I am satisfied. I just did not want Ivy to be worried about me. There was nothing she could do to help me that we could not do on our own. Our marriage is between us. I do not need my best friend to solve all of my problems for me like she used to do back in London. I am capable of solving my own issues now."

A pang of disappointment lowered Matthew's spirits, even though he should have anticipated her answer. "Aimee, can we talk?"

She turned her face against his chest but did not speak.

"Aimee. Look at me." He gently took her chin in his hand and turned her face to him.

Her beautiful green eyes searched his for several moments. "Where has talking ever gotten us?"

"I need you to listen to me."

"No, Matthew, I will not! You are always belittling me and… and I have had enough of it today."

Tears welled up in her eyes, and Matthew hated himself for making her cry. What a brute of a man he was. There had been far too many times just in their short marriage when he had made her cry. Was he not supposed to love his wife as Christ loved his church? He had failed their marriage from the start. "I promise I will not talk then, Aimee. Please, just let me hold you. Let me comfort you."

She seemed to think for a moment, no doubt desperate to find a reason to say no. But after a moment, she released a long sigh and all of the muscles in her body relaxed against him.

"Thank you, Aimee. Thank you, love." It scared Matthew that he had just used that term of affection in a serious manner. He chose to ignore the fear, however, as he smoothed her hair and held her tight as sobs racked her body. After the sun had begun to sink beyond the ocean and they were docked near the mainland, he still held her there. It felt so good to have this woman in his arms that he never wanted to let go.

"Matthew?" Her voice was hardly more than a whisper.

"What is it?" He smoothed some hair off of her face, nudging her back so he could see her face.

"Thank you."

"For what?" She had nothing to thank him for. He had been a terrible husband since their wedding day.

"For saving me. Every time I need you, you are right there. I...I know we do not love each other yet, but today I learned I want our marriage to work. I am sick and tired of being bounced from greedy man to greedy man back in London. I am sick of men like Eric. I never thought I would say this, but you are a good man. I want to truly begin again this time. I feel like we have known each other since we were children, but have never had the chance to become friends."

Relief warmed Matthew's stomach. "Aimee, I would love nothing more than that. Please, let's consider our stay here a honeymoon—or no, a time to court. We will forget about all of our past arguments and start again, like we are seeing each other for the first time."

Aimee offered him a gracious smile that sent butterflies fluttering through his entire body.

He bowed low and caught her hand in his. "Captain... Reverend Emery at your service, milady."

A giggle bubbled out of her.

"Whom do I have the pleasure of meeting?"

She shook her head slightly, but played along. "Mrs. Aimee Emery."

A part of him rejoiced that she had not introduced herself with her previous name. He knew how much she had valued her title of "lady." Perhaps this side trip to Charleston would be the best distraction that had happened to them.

Chapter 13

It was unnerving to be surrounded by a town full of people she had never met but would be living with for an undetermined amount of time. Aimee wished she had been able to meet Reverend Melville before they moved into his old home, but he had already been on his way back to London when they arrived to Charleston. The people of the town had not been expecting Matthew, as Reverend Melville had told them that he was not sure where Matthew was and if the letter would reach him in time.

Everyone in town had been relieved to have Matthew with them, and they had greeted them warmly. Several married couples had brought food over to the little house they were staying in, and they had enough meals to last them for a week. Aimee had told them that she had no idea how to cook, so a handful of women had offered to teach her how to make a couple recipes so she could get by. Aimee had never even thought of cooking for herself in her life in London. Someone had always been there to cook for her. No matter. Aimee had gotten her hands dirty on more than one occasion since her arrival in the Caribbean, and she was sure she would not mind cooking some meals. Learning might even be fun.

Matthew had let his crew go, but he still kept his ship. His crew was eager to get back to work and back to sea, and Matthew had said he was not sure when he would need to sail again. It was so strange to Aimee that she could be staying here for such a long time.

At least five families had offered them some additional comforts for their home. They now had some more cooking dishes and plates, and some gardening supplies. Mrs. Beecham, a kind woman from the congregation who only seemed a few years older than Aimee, had insisted on teaching her the art of gardening. Aimee chuckled at the very thought of it. She may have come a long way from her days in London, but she was certain she had no desire to garden in her future.

Life was quite simple in the Province of Carolina, Aimee had discovered. She might even be able to get used to it if she gave it a good chance.

***

Aimee could not believe it, but she decided she was happy to be spending a yet-to-be-determined amount of time in a new town, a new continent. It would help her start over here.

Matthew was taking their vow of new beginnings seriously. She had wanted to embrace him the other day, but he had insisted he would never embrace a woman he had known only a day. Now, they were settled in the little parsonage that had belonged to the reverend who had summoned Matthew.

Although they had already been living here for two weeks, Aimee wished she could make it feel more like a home. It was a tiny house, with one bedchamber and a kitchen. She was used to much grander surroundings, but she had vowed not to complain, as she was starting her life over. Who knew, maybe one day she could bring herself to purchase a simpler dress in town and wear it. Matthew would probably like that. Perhaps she would look for the most plain dress—maybe even something in an unfortunate color like *brown*—and wear it for him.

She glanced over at her husband, who was writing like a madman. His Bible lay open beside him, so she assumed he was re-writing one of the sermons she had destroyed. She hated that he slept out here on the settee. Of course, Aimee was not ready to fully become his wife, but she missed his company at night. No matter how much she hated it, she was glad he was being a perfect gentleman.

They had sent Eric packing on the first ship out of town. Relief flooded Aimee as she remembered seeing him retreat. They would never have to worry about him interfering with their marriage again.

She moved over to her husband's side and touched his arm. "Won't you go to sleep already, Matthew? It is quite late."

"This is important. I have my first service tomorrow, and I want to make a good impression on my congregation."

"I understand. Please, just make sure you get enough sleep tonight. You do not need to be up there preaching with dark circles under your eyes. What will the congregation think?" Aimee winked so he knew she was only teasing him. "I will be sitting right there. You can look at me when you speak, because you already know how I feel about you. There will be no need to worry about the rest of the congregation."

"I will get rest soon, Aimee. Go on to bed. I will look forward to seeing you tomorrow morning."

* * *

Matthew poked his head in the bedroom door to make sure his wife was asleep before he doused the lamp. Aimee lay sound asleep, wrapped in a pile of blankets. Moonlight streamed in from the window above her, illuminating her loose blond curls. A slight, peaceful smile lightened her face. There was no way he could deny that God had blessed him with a beautiful wife. "Goodnight, wife."

He silently closed the door behind him before moving to his makeshift bed. Matthew was not sure how the Aimee would react to his sermon tomorrow, but he wanted her to hear it so she knew he cared about her.

He had thought long and hard before choosing a subject that his new congregation would connect to, but he realized God had given him a different, dearer audience first and foremost. Aimee needed someone to remind her that her appearance, while it was beautiful, was not what mattered most.

Matthew laid back on the settee and pulled the blanket up to his chin. He prayed Aimee would not take his sermon too personally and get upset with him for his choice.

* * *

Chapter 13

The next morning, Aimee rose early to make sure she looked nice enough to be seen in front of Matthew's church-goers. She wanted to make a good impression on them, and she knew of no other way than what she had been taught back home. Aimee sat in the center of the front pew as she had promised Matthew. About twenty people stood lined up behind her, making this congregation much smaller than she was used to back in London. The church was modest, but well-kept. Really, it was interesting to be in such a wildly different setting from what she was accustomed to.

Matthew looked so fetching up there at the pulpit in his robe that Aimee had trouble concentrating on the service. She smiled and shook her head. How differently she would have been thinking if she had stayed at home in London!

She had come far in the past month. Earlier, she had declared this man her worst foe. And now, they were married. If Aimee was honest with herself, she would admit that she was almost… happy.

The thought did strange things to her insides, so she decided to stop thinking about it and focus on his sermon instead.

"So many people I have met believe that their appearance is the most valuable part of them. But they are wrong." Matthew's eyes locked with hers and he paused. "God looks at the *hearts* of His children."

Blood rushed straight to Aimee's cheeks. Had he really felt the need to write a sermon about her? Hot tears welled up in her eyes. How long must he have been going on about her to everyone, while she was sitting here, daydreaming? This was humiliating. Why, it was the most mortifying moment of her life! Here he was, preaching about her private life in front of all of these people they barely even knew!

"I know someone very dear to me who believed that her appearance..."

Aimee was not able to hear the rest of Matthew's sentence as she shot up from the pew and sped toward the exit without one look behind her. How *dare* he make an example of her?

She had never made such a ghastly public display, but would it have been any better to start screaming in the middle of her husband's sermon? No, this was the wiser choice. She ran around to the back of the church—where she was certain no concerned church-goers would find her—and sat down on a large rock.

It hurt that Matthew still thought so little of her. She had not done one vain thing since they had decided to start over, and here he was bringing up her past. To an entire congregation of strangers, no less! Why, the nerve of this man.

She was beginning to doubt they would ever be able to truly start over. He would always see her as the *vain princess.*

The crunch of boots walking on crushed stone alerted Aimee that someone had followed her out to her hiding place. "Please, leave me be. I simply needed a moment alone to get fresh air. I am all right. I will be back soon. There is no need to worry about me."

"Aimee, who else do you think followed you outside?"

She squeezed her eyes shut. The fool had stopped his own sermon just to go bother her? What would the people think of him now? "Go back to your congregation." A hand touched the small of her back, startling her so much that she almost fell off of the rock she was perched on. Matthew was quick to catch her before he knelt on the ground in front of her.

"What is wrong?" His eyes were so concerned, so big and blue. How dare he play the innocent?

Well, maybe he was just stupid. She could deal with that. "Matthew, you know that you went up there and preached about how much you dislike me in front of all of those people?"

"Darling…"

"Don't call me that when you do not mean it!" She quickly got to her feet, feeling only some vindication when her skirts hit into his face. "I am so weary from all of your false sweetness. You said we would forget our pasts, Matthew. And what do you do? You stand up there and preach to all of these strangers about what a terrible person I am. Well, if that's how you see me, as a spoiled, vain, little brat, I apologize. I can't wait until we get back to London. My father will *hate* you. He will make sure that I will never have to see you again, I can assure you of that."

"Aimee, please, just listen to me." He grabbed her hands in his, standing up in front of her. "You are not wrong. I wrote that about someone I *used to know*. Someone who has changed. You are a different person now, and so am I. I hope you know that. I beg your forgiveness for all the times I acted like I don't have flaws of my own. I have been a terrible husband to you. I used to judge people the moment I saw them. I still struggle with sins, and I know I always will. I am no better than you, darling. And I mean it when I call you *darling*. I beg your forgiveness for the times I have acted like I was superior."

"Why do you care about me, Matthew?" If his answer was something like it was his duty because she was his wife, she would swear then and there that she would leave him and never return.

He stood there fidgeting with his hands and his robe for a few moments, silent. He looked back and forth between her and the door to the church. No doubt he thought this was not the time or the place to hold this discussion, but Aimee knew that it was far more important than how fast he got back to his congregation.

"I want an answer right now. I grow tired of playing this game with you, wondering how we are going to feel about each other each day. I'm tired of not being sure whether my husband likes me or hates me. I cannot live in confusion another day." Aimee was so frustrated she wanted to scream. She wondered when the letter she had written to her father on her wedding day would arrive home. A lot had changed since those words were written, and yet so much had not.

"Aimee." He tugged her hand free from fidgeting with her dress and held it still in his. The warmth seeped onto her fingers, and she could not seem to focus on anything but the feeling of his big hand wrapped around hers. "I care about you because you are my best friend. I don't think there is a moment in the day when I am not thinking about you. You are much cleverer than anyone gives you credit for, and you are good, and so caring. You try to see the best in others, especially when I don't. I admire you deeply, Aimee, and I daresay I love you."

With each word the man spoke, tears formed in her eyes. This had not been what she expected. For goodness sake, she had just been preparing herself to move back to England with her father. She had never thought that Matthew could grow to love her. "I…I do not know what to say."

"I'm not expecting you to say anything." He leaned close and kissed her cheek. "Come now, let's go back to the congregation."

Aimee let Matthew help her to stand, his arm around her waist. He strolled back to the entrance of the church. "Are you ready, dear?"

Aimee knew she would never be ready, but she nodded nonetheless. All heads turned straight to the back of the church. She ignored the people's prying eyes and continued onward. Goodness, this was embarrassing, but Aimee knew it was best in the end to confront what she had done.

Finally, she was back in her pew. Moments later, Matthew was back at the pulpit. He smiled shyly. "Please excuse us for the interruption. We appreciate your patience."

Heat stung Aimee's cheeks, but she ignored it. She had brought this embarrassment on herself. She was startled when someone sat next to her. Mrs. Beecham. "Are you all right, Mrs. Emery?" She whispered.

Aimee nodded. It felt good to be genuinely cared about. The woman patted her hand and then focused her attention on Matthew. Aimee realized it was time she did the same, grateful that the congregation seemed to move past their concern over her actions.

Chapter 14

❦

Several weeks had passed, and Matthew's feelings had only grown since that Sunday afternoon. He was certain he and Aimee had set a personal record of days they had spent without an argument.

He wiped sweat from his brow, scowling up at the midday sun. Although the weather was still pleasant, it was becoming fall soon, and they would need firewood to supply them through the winter. Matthew had never chopped firewood before, having lived in the center of London and on a ship his entire life, but he was starting to get the hang of it. He had done a lot of manual work on the ship, so he found he had adjusted well.

Aimee walked in front of him, forcing him to stop mid-swing. She made a charming figure, flour stuck to her face and an apron tied about her waist. Matthew chuckled at the sight and set his axe down. "Come here, dear." He pulled her close and brushed the flour from her cheek before kissing her there.

"Matthew, I am going into town to get my dress altered, all

right?"

The thought of his wife going into town alone bothered him, but he was tied up for the rest of the afternoon with some congregation members who had requested a visit from him. "Are the ladies from church going with you? I want you to stay safe." She had befriended a small group of married women who chatted with her after church every Sunday. After hearing about how Aimee had ended up in the area, they had even donated some dresses for her, but most were too large on her slender frame.

"I am meeting Mrs. Beecham at the tailor's. She wanted me to go hat shopping with her after. It has been years since she has been to England, and she does not know the latest fashions, so she requested that I assist her. It might be getting dark by the time we are done, but I am certain she will have someone drop me off back at home. You won't have to worry about me."

"I do not want you going there unescorted, Aimee. I know we don't have any staff to take you around like you did back home, but it is a long walk for a woman alone. I do not want you to get hurt. I hope you understand that I am not being unreasonable." Matthew gathered the small pile of wood he had chopped and placed it under the awning of their front porch.

"I am capable of handling myself, husband." She jutted out her little chin, following him to the porch.

He resisted the urge to retort that she obviously was not able to handle herself, because she got herself abducted in Port Royal, but he decided it was not worth it to break their streak of peace. He knew she remembered what had happened in Port Royal, so there was no need to remind her. God would take care of Aimee. Besides, Matthew knew there was nothing he could do to stop her. Aimee was an independent woman, and while she might listen to Matthew's opinion, she could and would do what she wanted in the end. "All right, wife. I will see you at dinner tonight." He pulled her close and stole a quick, chaste kiss.

Her face broke into a sweet grin and she squeezed him in a short hug. "Thank you for not arguing. I will be back before you know it!"

She flittered away and down the path, her golden hair bouncing onto her shoulders with each step she took. Matthew could not believe the oversized dress she was wearing. It was brown, of all colors. While he appreciated her newfound modesty, he was going to miss her beautifully colored gowns. Maybe he would be able to save enough money to buy her one for Christmas. She had altered her life rather drastically in a short amount of time, but Matthew had rather liked some of her old ways.

After Aimee was out of sight, he leaned his head against the front porch railing and said a quick prayer for her safety on her journey in the city.

Goodness, he had almost forgotten about the visits he had to pay today. One member of the congregation had broken his leg and was unable to attend church for a long while, and another family was struck with a sickness. He had to visit the shut-in members before dinner time and it was already getting late. Suddenly, all Matthew could do was look forward to dinner when he would see Aimee once again.

* * *

The cool autumn air was filled with the tap-tap of horses' hooves, the creak of wagon wheels, the chatter of people, and the hawking of sellers on the town square. Civilization. Sometimes Aimee forgot how much she had missed this while she was at sea. It was so refreshing to see people whose faces she did not recognize. It reminded her of home. Scents of stew and cool, salty sea air and horse assaulted her nose. While it was not pleasant, anything was better than the stench of the bilge. Even though she had washed her hair several times since their return to land, sometimes Aimee still thought she could smell the awful scent upon her. She feared it would cling to her throughout the rest of her time in this town.

It felt good to be a part of urban life again, there was no denying that. The town was much smaller than her home of London, but it was more civilized than the Caribbean islands she had visited with Matthew. To her, it was a happy medium, so she could not complain.

A child scurried in front of her, kicking a ball his friend was chasing. Aimee laughed with them when they skidded to a stop to avoid running into a stout, suited man outside of the general store. Still laughing, Aimee turned down a side street that led to the tailor's shop. Mrs. Beecham had shown her this shortcut the last time they had been in town together.

The children giggled and dodged the man before continuing along their way. It felt good to see children enjoying life.

In her laughter, Aimee did not notice a group of teenage boys until she bumped right into one of them. They seemed to have popped up from nowhere.

"Oh. I am sorry, sir. Excuse me." Aimee backed up a step, intending to move out of their way.

The three young men circled around her while the fourth

glared at her, fire in his turquoise eyes. A twinge of fear ignited in Aimee's stomach. She had meant no harm to these boys. "I am sorry." She tried to take the annoyance out of her tone, but they really were getting in her way. "I was not paying attention to where I was going. It was my mistake, if you will forgive me." What else did they want from her but an apology? They were blowing this situation way out of proportion.

"What is your name, little lady?" The young man she had run into moved a few steps closer. Although he was in his teens, he still towered over her by a head or so, and his shoulders were wide enough to make him look like a man.

Fear tightened Aimee's throat. Not again. She refused to allow herself to be cornered by men again. Besides, she had promised Matthew she would be safe.

"I do not comprehend why it concerns you, but if you must know, m-my name is Aimee Emery." She tried to slide past him and run to safety, but he caught her wrist with an iron, vise-like grip. "And...and my husband is a reverend here in town, so once he hears you have detained me, he will ensure that you are strictly punished for your actions. He is well-admired around here, and many people will support him."

"Now, what are you talkin' about what we are goin' to be doin' to you? All we are doin' is lookin', ma'am. No harm in that." The man who was apparently their mouth and their brains pointed at her loose brown dress. His compatriots jeered at her, stepping closer. "So, does your husband refuse to buy you new clothes? You could do so much better in something that would...flatter your figure." He gestured to her body, and without even a groping touch, he made Aimee feel ugly and naked. And angry.

"How dare you question me? My clothing choices are none

162

of your business. Now, I demand you release me at once."
Aimee tried to jerk herself away from him.

"Go ahead and make me release you, little spitfire." He
wrenched her arm behind her back. Pain crept down her spine
as the air *wooshed* out of her lungs.

"Get your hands off of me *this instant!*" Aimee struggled
against his grip, but he had immobilized her with her arm
behind her back. Her back felt as if it had been stabbed all
along its length with a thousand daggers.

Another man, this one a bit older, grabbed one of her legs
as she kicked them into the air. Luckily, she kicked hard
enough to lessen their grip. He leaned close to her, undeterred,
brushing a finger against her cheek. He turned back to the
group. "Go home, boys, and I will save you the embarrassment
of being overpowered by a little woman. I will teach some
sense to this strumpet on my own."

She let her body go limp as the man watched the other young
men exit the alleyway. This was good. Now, there was only
one man to fight. She had to time everything perfectly, or
she would be ruined for certain. The man pinned her back
against the brick wall of the alley, moving her twisted arm
above her head. It was all Aimee could do not to cry out in
pain, but she would not give him the satisfaction of knowing
he had hurt her. He leaned close in an effort to steal a kiss, but
she turned her head and he missed, kissing the wall instead.
He growled in disapproval. "You ungrateful little whore...I'll
teach you a lesson." He raised his arm as if to backhand her,
but Aimee caught his elbow with her free hand before his hand
made contact with her face. Although he was stronger than
her, Aimee took his moment of confusion to her advantage.
She rammed her knee up between his legs.

With a hiss of pain, the man finally released her to brace himself. Aimee took a moment to debate whether to run or try to fight him off further. There was no way she could get away fast enough in her oversized dress. She would trip and fall on her face, and then he would catch up to her. No, she needed to defend herself. After taking a moment to check her surroundings, she noticed an iron crowbar next to a crate on the other side of the alley. If only she could get her hands on that...

Just as she was about to launch herself toward the weapon, the man lunged at her. His grip was tighter this time, more violent. Great. Rather than distracting him, she had incensed him further. She opened her mouth to scream for help, but he slammed a hand across her lips. Her teeth cut into her lips due to the sudden pressure, and the metallic taste of blood entered her mouth.

Oh God, please help me here. Surely I was not saved by Matthew months ago from a situation like this just to be taken again. Aimee bit the palm of his hand as hard as she could and rammed her head back against his.

"Help!" she screamed as she ran for the crowbar. This time, she had the heavy object in her grasp just as the man came upon her again. She hefted it up and hit him across the knees. One of his legs gave out and he stumbled to the ground. Aimee took the opportunity to raise the crowbar over her head, ready to bring it down on him and end the chase for good.

"I do believe you have done enough damage already, darling. I don't think he can walk anymore."

Aimee must have lost her mind, because she was nearly certain she had just heard her husband's voice.

Suddenly, Matthew stood at the end of the alley, a slight grin turning up a corner of his mouth.

In her surprise, Aimee dropped the crowbar. It crashed onto the man's head anyway, rendering him thoroughly unconscious.

"Well, I suppose that will do it."

In shock, Aimee looked from the man she had just defeated to her husband. Matthew ran to her side, his arms open wide. "We need to stop running into each other like this." He tugged her against his chest, a laugh vibrating in his chest against her cheek.

After an embrace, Matthew knelt down to check on the man. "He's breathing, but you knocked him out. He'll be gone for a while."

"You have to admit, this time I handled myself quite well. I took care of them without your help." Aimee started laughing even as tears sprung in her eyes. She blinked them back. It was useless to cry now, when the action was over.

"Oh darling, what happened here?" His hand ran in comforting circles against her back. She breathed in his strong, cedar scent and reveled in the comfort that was his arms.

"I am not certain, Matthew. One moment, I was walking to the tailor's shop, and the next, I was surrounded by this band of men...young men...almost teenage boys, actually. They would not let me go, and they asked me my name. Some of them left, but the last man held me back."

"I will ask around town and see that they are found."

"No, it is not worth the trouble. They just frightened me; they did not hurt me. I am afraid I hurt them worse than they did me." She only allowed herself to smile slightly as she looked down at the unconscious man. "Most of the boys left right away, anyway. The last man here...he is older, and stronger."

He patted a lock of her hair behind her ear. "What did they want from you?"

"I-I am not certain. I would suppose they wanted what the men back in Port Royal wanted from me."

Aimee had to admit that it was odd that men like those had struck at full daylight and had not even touched her purse, but she did not want to concern Matthew further. It was just an odd coincidence, and she was safe now, so there was nothing for them to worry about.

"Let's get you to the tailor's shop, all right?" He pulled away from her ever so slightly. "That is, if you still wish to go. I am certain Mrs. Beecham would understand if you rescheduled your meeting with her. I would be happy to take you home after I turn this man into the constable."

"I don't mind meeting Mrs. Beecham this afternoon. And you do not have to escort me. The tailor's shop is just around the corner." She paused. "Or were you not busy for the rest of tonight?"

"The people from church can wait, darling. You are the most important member of my congregation to me."

"All right, I will allow you to escort me, but only so you do not worry about me."

A smile brightened his clear blue eyes. "Let's go meet Mrs. Beecham, then."

Chapter 15

ꙮ

Aimee giggled as Mrs. Beecham recounted the tale of her engagement from the other side of the dressing curtain. Mr. and Mrs. Beecham had met when they were children, and he had told her he wanted to marry her when they were only five years old. She clearly remembered laughing at him and throwing sand in his face before running away. Fifteen years later, Mr. Beecham convinced her to meet him on the beach and proposed to her there with the reassurance that he would not mind if she threw sand at him.

Aimee adored a good love story, and she was happy that Mrs. Beecham was sharing hers with her. Matthew was in the other room and out of earshot, so they were taking the opportunity to talk about life as married women.

"I wish I knew what it is like to be engaged. I skipped that part of marriage!" Aimee tugged the sleeve of her newly fitted dress up her arm.

Mrs. Beecham eyed her suspiciously from the other side of the curtain. "I am certain you two were not immediately close from your first day of marriage. And you have grown closer. That is a good step to make, Mrs. Emery."

"Well, I suppose that is true. But I would not call that our engagement. We never really courted, either. We just went straight to marriage."

"Oh, Mrs. Emery, I am sorry about that." Mrs. Beecham assisted Aimee with the buttons on the back of her dress.

"I am as well." Aimee closed her eyes. "Mrs. Beecham, how did you know…I pray you will excuse me for this forward question, but…how did you know you loved your husband when he proposed to you? How did you know you would be happy together?" She found herself looking up to this woman, who was not much older, yet seemed so much more experienced, with her loving husband and two children, and a third on the way.

"I think every relationship is different, Mrs. Emery. There is not always a tried and true way to know you are in love. It just so happens that when you spend enough time with a person and you grow to respect them, and there are feelings there that you can't quite explain….well, I call that love. I call being happy to see David every day love. I call wanting to be his alone forever love. And…don't worry if you are not feeling those emotions right now. I know plenty of couples who either did not love each other right away, or took a while to be happy together. And as I am certain you know, many marriages do not even find love." She buttoned the last button on Aimee's gown and turned her around. "But I suspect you do not have to worry about that, because I have seen the way the two of you look at each other."

Heat stained Aimee's cheeks and she had to look away for fear of Mrs. Beecham seeing the tears in her eyes. Could she love Matthew? And could it be so obvious? "I am not certain what to think anymore, Mrs. Beecham. Oh, what should I do?"

"I cannot tell you what to feel. That is up to you to decide."

Aimee brushed her hands across her face, trying desperately to clear her mind. She was baffled by the feelings she was having for Matthew as of late. If she loved him and he loved her, then…was their marriage never a mistake? Could it have been a blessing? What would their life be like if that was so?

For over a month after her marriage, she had done nothing but regret it. Perhaps she should have looked on the bright side of things. Maybe they would have a much more pleasant relationship if she had not been so selfish.

Aimee pushed those thoughts from her head and turned to look in the long dressing mirror. Her new dress was beautiful. The tailor had declared her plain brown dress unusable, but said he had something in the back for her—a gift from him to the new preacher and his wife. This dress fit her modestly without being frumpy. It was a pretty pink color that brought out the pink in her cheeks. Pure white lace adorned the edges. It lacked the shiny, flashy aspects that Aimee once sought, but it was the perfect combination of Aimee's style and her newfound modesty.

"Oh, I love it! Don't you, Mrs. Beecham?" Aimee twirled around, reveling in the feel of soft, clean skirts around her ankles. Oh, how it made her miss her full wardrobe from home.

"Yes, it is lovely. The color compliments your pretty green eyes. Let's go see what the reverend thinks of it, shall we?"

Aimee suddenly felt nervous as they approached Matthew, though she did not know why. Why should she care if he did not like her new dress? The man had no fashion sense, and she had been choosing her own gowns since her tenth birthday. Besides, it would not be the first time Matthew would disapprove of her clothing.

As if to spite her low expectations of him, Matthew jumped to his feet the moment she entered the room. "Aimee." A smile turned up the corners of his lips as he admired her gown. Aimee suddenly felt shy. "I do hope that you like your new dress. It becomes you more than I can say."

"Oh, Matthew, it is perfect. I am so happy that you like it."

"I am glad you found something you like. I think it is perfect as well. Now, let's get ready to return home, shall we? Perhaps we still have time to make one of my calls before dinner time if you feel up to joining me."

"I think that is a grand idea, Matthew." Aimee squeezed her husband's hand as a realization struck her. "After what happened today, I do not want to be apart from you for long. I will see what I can do to help while you are making your calls."

Matthew smiled. "Thank you, Aimee."

Chapter 16

Aimee sat across from her brothers at the dining table. The food on her plate was expensive, but cold. Everyone around her was finished eating, but it was as if she had no appetite. She pushed her fork around on her plate. A man that she could not recognize sat at her side, his arm tight around her shoulders. She did not know anything about her situation except the lurking feeling of dread that hit her.

"Aimee, how about a kiss for your husband, hmm?" The nondescript man next to her pulled her straight off her chair and onto his lap before smothering her with a kiss.

Aimee's mind went straight back to her time in London. The men she had involved herself with had been fond of stealing kisses from her, even when she was not the most willing participant. Next, her memory flashed to her encounter with Eric Honeysett. She shoved the mysterious man away, tears streaming down her face.

"Where is Matthew? I want to see my husband! I demand you let me speak with him." She shot away from the man in her chair, the sudden movement shocking her brothers across the table.

"Little Aimee, your husband is right beside you. Are you well?" Pierre, her brother peered over at her.

"And who is this Matthew? Are you speaking of that horrible Mr. Emery?" Bernard's voice rang in the mix.

"Why are you talking about that man now? We have not spoken of him in years." Andre laughed softly, finishing his glass of wine and reclining back in his chair.

"Aimee, my sweet, go lay down. No doubt you are stressed and tired from taking care of the children, so you are not speaking in your right mind. It is not uncommon to feel stressed so soon after the birth of your little ones." Sebastien, her other brother, approached her and grabbed her elbow.

Normally, Aimee was close to Sebastien, but she pulled her arm away. He was talking nonsense. "Children? What children? Where is Matthew?"

"Aimee, we made sure Matthew was far away after you sent for us. You know that. You will never have to see him again. Goodness, it has been years, Aimee. What made you think of him all of a sudden?" Sebastien shrugged his shoulders at the mysterious man that Aimee supposed was her husband, and the father of her children.

Sickness soured her stomach.

"I love him, Sebastien. I need to see Matthew."

Laughter filled the room. Her brute of a husband shot up and pulled her from her brother with a violent tug. "I will have no such talk in my house, wife. What would the children think if they heard you speak like that?"

Aimee jabbed her elbow into the clingy man's ribs and ran away, ran down the hall, ran outside, ran as far as she could go...

Aimee awoke with the beginning of a scream in her throat and tears streaming from her eyes. She jumped out of bed and scurried to her bedroom door, unable to catch her breath. The door creaked as she opened it, but she was relieved to find Matthew sound asleep on the couch, his handsome, blond hair tousled and his arms splayed to either side of his body.

Thank you, God. It was just a silly, stupid nightmare that her worried mind had fabricated. She was still with Matthew. She was not married to a nameless brute, and she had no anonymous children.

Her tears slowing, Aimee returned to her bedroom and went back to her bed. She knew where the nightmare had come from, and she was not happy about it. A month ago, Aimee had penned a frantic letter to her brothers and her father, begging for them to come rescue her from Matthew. She feared more than anything that they would find her now and do exactly as she had once asked. Her father would never approve of the marriage.

Aimee needed to talk to a friend, but hated that it was far too late to call on Mrs. Beecham. Instead, she tucked herself back into bed and waited impatiently for daylight to arrive.

* * *

Matthew sipped some tea at the table of Mr. Lewis, the town's constable. There was no way he was going to allow Aimee's encounter with the group of boys in town go unnoticed. Those hooligans had to be punished, and Mr. Lewis was just the man to help Matthew track them down.

"How can I help you, Reverend Emery?" Mr. Lewis poured a good amount of cream into his tea as he spoke.

Matthew was not sure how to address this. "To put it plainly,

Mr. Lewis...my wife was attacked yesterday."

Mr. Lewis slammed his teacup back onto its saucer. "Your wife? Is she all right? Where is she?"

"Yes, Mr. Lewis, Aimee is all right. But she was surrounded by a group of teenage boys yesterday, and they tried to assault her. They seemed to want something from her specifically, because they asked her name. Aimee took care of them, though. One of the men ended up with a bad kneecap and a good-sized bump on his head, thanks to Aimee."

Mr. Lewis chuckled. "That's quite the force of a wife you've got there, Reverend. All right. I will be on the lookout for those boys to see if we can get to the bottom of this. It sounds quite suspicious to me."

"Thank you, Mr. Lewis. We deeply appreciate your assistance."

"It is my duty to the community, Reverend. And the least I can do to thank you for your service in the church. I will contact you as soon as I find out more about this case."

* * *

Aimee sat across from Mrs. Beecham at the table in her small home.

"What do you mean, you might have to call it off? Aimee, what are you talking about? He's your husband!" Mrs. Beecham added a lump of sugar to her tea and stirred it vigorously.

"Mrs. Beecham, it is not my choice—I may have no choice. I am not the same person I was when I got married. I...I was

174

selfish, and vain, and rude, and so, so childish."

"What does that have to do with now? Aimee, you are a changed person. I know that. Reverend Emery knows it too, for goodness sake." Mrs. Beecham grabbed her hand from across the small table. "So what is wrong?"

Aimee dropped the cookie she had been about to eat back onto her plate. "I did something horrible." She inhaled, trying to obtain the strength she needed to reveal what she had done. "I have not spoken about this to anyone. Not even Matthew. Directly after I married him, I wrote a lengthy letter addressed to my father and older brothers back home in London. I begged for them to come rescue me. I demanded that they help me get an annulment, and I told them that life with Matthew is intolerable."

"If they do find you here, Aimee, what do you think they will do? They cannot force you to annul your marriage…especially after you have been married for a while. There should be nothing to worry about, you silly thing."

"No. I know my family, Mrs. Beecham. First of all, they despise Matthew. They have hated him ever since his first day at our church back home when he was a boy. They knew about his past, so they hated him for it. They will never be happy with our match. My father was hoping for me to marry a rich man with a title…compared to that, in my father's eyes…Matthew is nothing." Aimee resisted the tears that threatened to cloud her vision.

"But you are married to him. I am not accustomed to life in London anymore, but, last I knew, it would ruin you to get a divorce. And Reverend Emery's career as a preacher would be over before it even started. I am certain your family would not want to bring that devastation upon you."

Matthew poked his head inside the door. His sudden appearance startled Aimee. She prayed he had not heard much of their discussion. She did not need him worrying about what would happen if her father responded to the letter. After all, he may not even reply, and then there would be nothing to worry about. "Mrs. Beecham, your husband is here."

"Oh, already! I am afraid I must be going, dear Mrs. Emery. I wish you Godspeed in everything we discussed." Mrs. Beecham patted Aimee on the wrist and exited through the door Matthew had held for her.

"Aimee." Egad, had he heard her? What did he intend to speak to her about?

"Yes?"

"Come here." He pulled her close, his arms winding around her waist. "We need to talk."

Oh dear.

"Shall we sit down?" He motioned for the settee, allowing her to sit before he positioned himself next to her.

"Matthew, what is the matter? You are frightening me." Aimee tried to laugh the situation away, but Matthew's hard gaze offered no amusement.

"Those boys attacked you, Aimee." He paused, searching her face. "They were not just a band of ruffians. They were paid to kidnap you."

* * *

Matthew tried to gauge his wife's reaction as he relayed the dark news to her. Her face tightened a little bit, but he had to admit he was proud of her. She put on a brave front for someone who should be frightened. "Why…why were they paid to kidnap me? Who paid them?"

"I have not found out yet. One of the men from my crew still in town tracked down one of the boys. He was only seventeen years old. He would not say who paid him or why, but he confirmed that he had…" Emotion choked Matthew's voice for a moment. "He had been watching you for a few weeks, Aimee. We never even noticed this boy following you. I do not know how or why, but he knew that you were going to the tailor's at the time you were. And he and his group of friends were paid to capture you."

"Were they meant to harm me?" she said breathlessly.

Matthew took her hand in his and rubbed the back of it with his thumb. "I don't know, sweetheart. The constable tracked the boy down, but he could not get any more information out of him about who paid him or why he did it."

"That is odd."

"We need to be more cautious." Matthew wracked his mind for who in town could have wanted Aimee captured, but nothing came up. He did not know many people in town outside of his congregation. Aimee launched herself forward into his embrace. The sudden movement threw him off balance for a moment, but he quickly righted himself and patted his wife on the back. "I will do everything in my power to keep you safe, Aimee. But most importantly, I will be praying. There should be nothing to fear."

Chapter 17

⁂

Aimee adored the hymn they were singing at church. Singing had always been her favorite part of the services back home. Part of her enjoyed how it broke up what one might consider the monotony of the service, but she had always appreciated the chance it offered to praise God directly, rather than simply sitting there and listening to the reverend preach. Although, today, the reverend was quite captivating.

Matthew looked so much in his element up there, in front of the congregation. His breaths were smooth and calm. His face was so peaceful, so happy. His eyes met hers over the heads of the congregation and she noticed the trace of a smile on his lips. She smiled back, being mindful so Mrs. Beecham, who was seated next to her, would not notice.

God help her. She loved her handsome, stubborn preacher man. It was a terrifying and thrilling realization, and she could not wait until the service was over so she could tell him her realization. Nerves tingled in her stomach for reasons she could not quite explain. There was no reason to fear telling her husband she loved him—hadn't he expressed the same sentiments to her shortly ago?

The door in the back of the sanctuary slammed open. Aimee did her best to ignore it, although she was tempted to turn around and see who had sauntered into the service so late. Matthew would be proud of her concentration on his sermon.

Up at the altar, Matthew's eyes drifted to the back of the sanctuary. A coldness seemed to wash over his body, one that reached Aimee as well. His words slowed until they stopped coming from his mouth.

Aimee spun around, just in time to see her father and three of her brothers, Pierre, Anton, and Sebastien approach her pew. A wave of emotions crashed over her head. She was certainly happy to see her family again. There was no denying that. But she also felt confusion, apprehension, and maybe just a little fear at the sight. After all, they had come all this way—all the way across the sea—to save her from a marriage…that she was happy with now. It was if her nightmare was coming into fruition. Oh, this could not go well.

"Aimee, my pet." Her father pulled her up from the pew and embraced her. His familiar, citrusy scent washed over her, bringing comfort immediately. It had been so long since she had last hugged her father. Tears moistened her eyes, but she quickly composed herself.

"Papa." Aimee pulled away, suddenly very aware that Matthew had stopped preaching and the congregation was staring at her and her family. "We must move outside. I hate to disturb the church service." Aimee nodded at her husband, trying to communicate to him that it would be fine to stay here and finish the sermon while she spoke to her family outside.

Anton, Pierre, and Sebastien filed outside before Aimee and her father, nodding at the people who lined the pews as they passed. That was just like her family to have no second thought about being the center of attention. Aimee wanted to hide underneath her pew and pretend she was not involved in this, but she followed her family out of the church.

"Where are Maman and Bernard?" She asked once they were on the steps outside the church. Her oldest brother was missing from the group, and she hoped her mother was doing all right.

"You know how ill Maman gets on ships, little Aimee. It is too much motion for her." Anton wrapped his arms around her. "Bernard stayed with her."

"We all know Bernard just stayed back because he is trying to court that little lady he has had his eye on since last spring." Sebastien chuckled as he pulled Aimee into a bear hug.

"We were worried sick about you ever since you left to find your friend and only told Sebastien about your departure. Has that degenerate Emery harmed you, little Aimee?" Pierre took his turn to hug her.

"We cannot call him a degenerate, Pierre. He was preaching in there. He must not be too horrible, if they let him have a congregation." Sebastien playfully hit his brother's shoulder.

"We know about his past, boys. What he is doing now offers him no redemption." Father stepped forward. Blast, she had been hoping her father might not remember her husband's dark beginnings.

Aimee was ready to scream at them for all of the gossiping they were doing in front of her about her own husband.

"Aimee, I do not know where that man has been keeping you, but if you direct us there, we can pack up your things for you and get you out of here by nightfall." Anton gestured to the carriage that was waiting at the end of the pathway in front of the church. They had rented a carriage and horses? Goodness, her father was spending far too much money on this unneeded rescue mission.

"That is if she has anything. Did he sell all of your dresses or something? Why are you wearing this plain gown?" Pierre leaned closer, as if to inspect the quality of the fabric of her dress.

"I think it looks nice on her," Sebastien offered.

"Goodness, why are you so tan, little Aimee? Does he have you working outside?"

"My things are at our house, but I am not going anywhere with you all today."

"We can get you out by tonight, my pet." Her father patted her on the arm.

"But what about Matthew?"

"What about him? You will get an annulment and we will forget this whole misfortune happened." Anton answered as if Matthew was the most dispensable thing in the world. Now that Aimee thought about it, that seemed to be how her family treated everyone they considered lower in society's rank.

"I made a mistake when I wrote you that letter. I am so sorry that I caused you all to come here to save me from my marriage to Matthew, but I do not need rescuing anymore." Aimee moved her family to the back side of the church, worried that the congregation might overhear their conversation if they exited the building. She was thankful that Matthew had gotten the hint and stayed inside. She had already made herself a spectacle one too many times at this church.

The men all stood in silence, staring at her. After a few long moments, Pierre burst out into laughter. Her other brothers followed suit.

"She is teasing us, right?" Anton wheezed between bouts of laughter.

Aimee thwacked him upside the head with the side of her hand. "I am not teasing you. I am being completely serious. I am so thankful you all came for me, but there is no need to take me home. I will stay here with my husband."

"Your husband? My little Aimee, we *will* get you an annulment. I will make certain that no one back home hears about this. We will still find you a fine husband. You do not need to fret about that. I have everything taken care of." Her father patted her on the arm.

"I already have a fine husband—"

"Aimee, that man has a horrible reputation. He is no good for you. You will be shunned by all of your friends. You will have no title, no money, nothing that you ever wanted." Pierre waved his arms as he spoke, obviously quite upset about her future. "That is not how you want to live, is it?"

* * *

As soon as he had finished his sermon and calmed his confused congregation, Matthew went out to find Aimee. He was astonished none of the men surrounding Aimee heard him approach. He recognized them from London as her father and brothers, the very men who had warned him to back away from Aimee when they were children. And their conversation did not seem to be going well.

"I do not care what people in London think about us. Matthew saved me from a terrifying situation, and he has taken good care of me since then."

Well, at least she does not hate me any longer.

"I know this might come as a shock to you, but I love him."

Was she serious? Matthew did not know what to make of that statement.

"I do not know what foolishness this man has been brain-washing you with, Aimee, but I do not believe that you actually love him," one of the older brothers stated matter-of-factly.

"I believe her," another brother muttered quietly. Matthew knew this one was the youngest, Sebastien. The man was about the same age as Matthew, if he recalled correctly.

"Aimee, you do not love him," her father interjected, shooting a glare at Sebastien.

"She—she's not with child, is she?"

That was enough. Matthew forced his way through the wall Aimee's brothers had built around her. "I will not have you talking about my wife this way."

One of the brothers slugged the one who uttered the unkind comment. Aimee's eyes jumped to Matthew's, and he could practically feel the frustration that was building up in her. Her cheeks were red and she looked about ready to scream.

"Apologize to your sister, Anton," her father demanded.

"I'm sorry, Aimee, it's just the only reason I could think of for you to be talking like this."

"I assure you that is not what has changed my feelings about Matthew."

Matthew was still reeling with the shock of her admission.

"Aimee, you are not sounding like yourself," Sebastien said.

"That is because I have had some changes of heart. But please, this is not the time or place to discuss this matter. Would you all like to come back to our house? I need to prepare a meal, but I can get that ready quickly and we can all discuss this then."

"Is he making you prepare your own food, Aimee?" Pierre sounded shocked.

"She doesn't even know how to cook," Anton said.

"I wanted to learn—I do not wish to discuss it further. Either you eat or you do not eat, it does not matter to me."

"All right, Aimee, we will join you for a meal, but I hope you start to see sense soon. I want to get to the bottom of this. Come along, dear." Her father offered her his arm.

"Father, there is no room for Mr. Emery in the carriage." Sebastien cast an apologetic look at Matthew.

"I will walk with Matthew." Aimee grabbed his hand and clung to it.

"Aimee, you are a lady, you are not going to walk—"

"I will do what I want. You cannot tell me what to do, Pierre."

"But it is not practical for a lady—"

"I have been walking back and forth to church with Matthew for a month now. I am certain I can handle myself." Aimee jutted her chin out as if she were daring any of her six-foot-and-up brothers to tell her otherwise. Matthew could not help but admire the way she bossed her big brothers around.

"Maybe that's why her skin has gotten so tan; she has been walking outside like some commoner," Anton retorted.

"Aimee, do you truly wish to walk?" her father questioned.

"Yes, Papa, I will walk home with my husband."

"Very well, then. Boys, we will let Aimee walk home."

After she offered her family some deliberately nondescript

directions on how to find her home, Aimee breathed a sigh of relief. She pressed close against Matthew's side as her family filed around the building and to the carriage, her brothers shaking their heads and glaring at Matthew. She entwined her hand with his and leaned even closer. "We need to get home before they do."

Matthew wrapped his arm around her waist as they walked. He wanted her brothers and father to know she was his and there was no way he would allow them to break their marriage apart, especially now that he knew she loved him. "Why?"

"You need to move your blanket and things from the sofa. I want them to think you have…" She paused, and her cheeks reddened. "I want them to think you have been sleeping in the bedroom all along."

"Oh. I…I uh, understand." Matthew's face heated at the thought. Truly, it was their only option. Her family seemed dead set on this marriage getting annulled, and Matthew was not sure what he could do to stop them. Aimee's father was a powerful man, and he always got what he wanted. A sick feeling weighed down his stomach. After all this time he had spent with Aimee, it would be devastating if they were forced to separate. However, he knew that if Aimee's father was insistent enough, he could ruin Matthew's career both in the church and in the merchant business. If those were destroyed, there was not much Matthew could do to support himself, much less his wife.

Dear God, please help us. You put us together for a reason, I am certain of that. It would be so unfitting to be separated like this after we have grown to love one another.

The walk to their home was short. Once they entered the house, Aimee rushed to put away his pillow and blankets in the bedroom. Matthew wondered where on earth the woman was planning on housing four grown men in their tiny home, but he knew now was not the time to question her.

Aimee's brothers and father entered without even knocking.

"Well, this place could certainly use improvement," her father muttered.

"I apologize, sir. We were not expecting company. This home was donated to us by the previous reverend who served here, and we are making by with what we have been given." Matthew stood up to his full height as he faced the man, determined not to show any signs of intimidation.

"Aimee, I cannot believe this man has been forcing you to cook for him. What has gotten into you, my child? You are a lady. Your mother and I raised you better than this."

Aimee stopped what she was doing in the kitchen to put her hands on her hips defiantly. "Papa, I enjoy cooking. Several of my friends from church taught me how to make some meals, and I enjoy doing it. We all eat, do we not? So how is it beneath us to cook the food we eat? Why is it someone else's job?"

Matthew's heart warmed at Aimee's statement. He had never been more proud of his wife. They had both changed so much since they were children in church together and he had judged her.

Aimee's family went silent as they walked around the small home, inspecting every inch of it. Matthew couldn't shake the feeling that it was not their home they were judging, but Matthew and his ability to care for Aimee.

Chapter 18

A imee resisted the urge to collapse to the floor when she closed the bedroom door behind her. She loved her brothers, but they were often difficult to handle, even if they thought they had her best interest in mind.

"You are wonderful with them." Matthew's voice startled her, although she was not sure how she could have forgotten he was in here. It was simply that he never spent much time in their...bedroom. He was loosening the buttons of his shirt, a half-smirk on his face. "I suppose you kept them on their toes when you were a little girl. I can just imagine you bossing them around. I never used to notice that when I saw you on Sundays."

The thought brought a smile to her face. It was true that she had bossed her big brothers around, but they had always had a soft spot for her, their only sister. Everything they did to her, they did out of love. She knew that, but sometimes it was difficult for her brothers to see past what they thought was right.

"Enough talk about your brothers, huh?" He offered her a crooked smile that made her heart skip a beat. He stepped closer.

Aimee bit her lip. She wanted to tell him what she had realized today. But what would he think of her? No matter, there was nothing she could do if he reacted irrationally. That would be his own fault. "Matthew, I have been meaning to…tell you something."

He immediately stilled. "What might that be?"

There was no easy way to do this. She had to just blurt it out. "I love you."

After a moment, his lips quirked upwards in a sheepish smile. "I heard you tell your family that…I was not certain if you truly meant it or if you just wanted them to leave you alone."

"No, I meant it." She studied her husband, wondering if it would be acceptable to change into her nightgown while he was in the room.

After a moment, he seemed to catch on to her thought. His face turned red. "I'll uh…I will turn my back."

Aimee inhaled sharply. "Matthew?"

He turned to face her again. "Yes?"

"When…when are we going to actually be married?"

His eyes grew larger. "You mean…"

Aimee nodded, closing the distance between them. "What do you think?" she whispered, wrapping an arm around his waist and resting her other hand on his shoulder. She rested her forehead against his collarbone.

"I think there is no better time than now, wife."

* * *

For the first time since she had met him, Aimee awoke before her husband did. Her cheek rested on his bare chest. This feel of his skin against hers was enough to flood her with memories of last night. She loved this man, and now there was nothing her father could do to separate them. Aimee had been around enough to know that a consummated marriage was a lot harder to break than a marriage of name only.

Aimee lazily traced her hand across the muscles of Matthew's chest and shoulders. Although he was not a large man, he was well sculpted from his days of sailing. She moved her hand up his neck, entangling it in his soft, light hair. He cleared his throat as his eyes opened. A smile slowly stretched across his face. "Good morning." He caught her hand in his and brought it to his lips.

"Even though I would like to stay here all day with you, I suppose I should get dressed. My family will be wanting breakfast."

Matthew leaned forward, engaging her in a kiss distracting enough to make her lay back down. "Your family can also learn to cook their own breakfast."

"I know. I just want to cook." She kissed him back before rising once again, this time to a full standing position before he could distract her again.

He jumped to his feet and made his way to the other side of the bed. "Allow me." Matthew snatched her robe from the dresser and held it out for her to wear. Aimee slid one arm through and then the next, relishing in the feel of her husband's hands on her shoulders. He pressed a soft kiss to her neck. "Aimee. I will not allow them to separate us. We will get through this." His kisses dropped lower, to her collarbone. "Together."

Her heart fluttered in her throat, responding to her husband's touch. "I pray so." She turned around and wrapped her arms around him. "Now let me go to my family."

"If you say so, *sweetheart*." A smirk lit his face as he used her nickname. "I will be out there in a moment."

Aimee was not at all surprised to see that her brothers and father were already awake and lurking suspiciously close to her bedroom door. She rolled her eyes at them and closed the door behind her so Matthew could get dressed in peace. "I trust that you slept well?"

They did not even make any effort to pretend they were not trying to listen in on her conversation with Matthew.

"Oh, we slept as well as we could…with the accommodations. The floor was quite crowded." Pierre stretched his shoulders.

"Be polite, Pierre. She gave us the best she could. It will not kill you to sleep on the floor for a couple of nights." Sebastien pulled Aimee into a hug. "Good morning, sister."

"Good morning, Sebastien." Aimee smiled. Sebastien had always been the level-headed brother. As the middle child, he had settled many a dispute between the other brothers. And no matter what, he had always sided with Aimee on every matter. Maybe he would be her ticket to getting her family to accept her marriage. If only she could get Sebastien alone later today to speak to him.

"I am going to make breakfast now, all right?"

"Aimee, you know how I feel about you cooking for us, but it isn't right. Please, allow me to hire you someone to do some of your household chores and your cooking. It is not your place to do such menial work." Her father grabbed her arm before she could enter the kitchen.

"Father, please. I do not wish to discuss this any further.

190

Now, do you want to eat something or not? Because that is what your choice is right now."

Aimee snatched her arm from her father's grasp and forced her way into the kitchen.

"With all due respect, I do not think you are going to find someone to cook your breakfast in time for today, sir." Matthew said as he leaned against the wall, his arms crossed as if daring someone to approach him. Aimee had to admit, she had never seen Matthew this confident or defiant in front of people like her family.

Her brothers remained silent as she prepared breakfast.

Chapter 19

A imee pulled Sebastien outside the second she could get him away from the others. She led him to the edge of the woods, to a stump underneath a leafy overhang. "What is going on with you, Am?" Sebastien settled down on the ground and motioned for Aimee to sit on the stump. "You certainly are not acting like yourself."

"Sebastien, I am not sure what has happened to me, but I know I am happy with Matthew here. Please understand that."

"I trust you, Am. I just want to understand why. You loved your home with us in London and the fine things we had there." Her brother rested his hand over hers comfortingly.

"As I am sure you know, I used to hate Matthew. But after he saved me in Port Royal…we were tossed together in a sense. And I had to get along with him, or my life would have been miserable. But after we started to get along together, I started to grow closer to him. Matthew and I have been through a lot together, Sebastien. God has worked some miracles in both of us. I have grown to love the person he has become. All I know is that I cannot bear for us to be separated." Unexpectedly, tears sprung into Aimee's eyes and her chest tightened. She bit her lip and tried to quiet a sob.

"Am...I believe you love him." Sebastien pulled her into his arms. "I will speak to Father about this. You know how he can get, but...in the end, I know he believes in love. You know he and Maman would have never married if it were not for love. So there has to be some kind of tenderness in his heart for that. He only wants to see that you are safe and that you love this man. As soon as he believes that you are happy, I am sure he will let things be."

"I pray you are right. I cannot bear to be separated from Matthew." *Especially after last night.* A sigh escaped her lips. "I love him, Sebastien. I could never live with myself if I married another man."

* * *

Matthew wanted to scream. He had barely survived his second day cooped up with Aimee's brothers and their constant interrogating. He was lucky he loved her, or he might have given in to their demands after the first day and he would be alone once again.

He leaned back against his pillow and lazily draped his arm over his wife's pillow as she joined him on the bed. "I can see where you get your stubbornness from, dear." She rolled her eyes as he offered her a wink.

A shadow crossed her face. "I wish I could meet *your* family, Matthew."

Something sank to the bottom of his stomach. It embarrassed him that she knew about his past. "I guarantee you that you are not missing anything. They were not the most genteel people. I'm sure they would have been rude to you, and you know they would be horrible for your reputation."

She slid next to him on the bed. "Everyone has good in them, Matthew. I believe your parents had some reasons to push them to what they did. And I am happy they existed, because without them, I would have never met you."

Matthew brushed a light kiss against her temple. "God has truly blessed us both, wife."

Her head nestled close to his chest. "You are right about that." She fell asleep with a smile on her face.

* * *

Matthew did not know what woke him. He felt a gentle, cool, night breeze from the window they had left open. It was comforting to smell a hint of the salty sea air. He did not know what he would do with himself if he had to live away from the sea for an extended period. It must have been cloudy outside, for no moonlight streamed through the window. The darkness was bewildering. He turned his back to it, facing his dear wife.

He slid his arm across the bed, expecting to find comfort in her soft warmth. But his hand hit nothing but cold air. Panic seized him, stealing the breath from his lungs. Matthew forced himself to inhale, scoffing at his silliness. His wife was out of bed; that was all. Her family's visit had left him on edge, so waking up alone was bound to make him worry for a moment. She was likely visiting the outhouse or couldn't sleep and was sitting in the kitchen to clear her mind. The woman would probably be back within moments, and when she returned, he decided he would give her a kiss and tell her how much he loved her. He would hold her and tell her that her family would never be able to separate them, so they had better realize it and return to London.

Despite everything his head told him, a niggling feeling of dread sat in his stomach. Shouldn't Aimee be back in bed by now? *God, please help me get over this constant worry. Everything is in Your control, and I need to remember that.* Still, no matter what he did, he could not shake the feeling. Matthew swung out of bed and lit a candle. Aimee would probably be annoyed with him for looking for her, but something inside him told him it was best to check.

She was not in their bedroom.

Matthew padded into the common area, where her father and her brothers lay sprawled out. They were all fast asleep, and there was no sign of Aimee.

She was not in the kitchen, either.

Matthew tried to keep their creaking front door silent as he went outside to find his wife. The fall air chilled him straight through his nightshirt. He wished he had grabbed his robe.

He paced around the house. She was not outside. Nausea hit him like a cannonball. If she wasn't here and her family was all still in the house, then what…

"Are you looking for your little wife?"

Matthew swung around. At the edge of the clearing, he could make out the tall figure of a man. But he did not need to see him to recognize that awful, deep, rasping voice.

Eric Honeysett had shown up just in time to make his life miserable.

He did not have time to question how the man had gotten back here so quickly or why he was dead set on ruining Matthew's marriage. If Aimee's family found out about Eric—a wealthy, handsome man with a high-class name—they could follow the man's lies blindly. "What have you done with her, Honeysett?" His voice was barely above a whisper.

"Aimee? She came with me quite peacefully. Right now, she is sound asleep in my bed." His blue-green eyes flashed with malice. "When are you going to face it, Emery? Your wife prefers me. And who can blame her?"

Matthew lunged, ready to grab the insufferable idiot and choke him until he gave a straight answer. "You stop speaking that nonsense right now, you unforgiveable little—"

"Ah, ah, ah, that's no way for a preacher to act." Honeysett reached a hand out to halt Matthew.

"I may be a preacher, but I am Aimee's husband first. If you hurt her, I swear—"

Eric's hands flew up as if he were innocent. "I have not hurt her. As I said a moment ago, she came with me quite peacefully."

Matthew clenched his jaw. "I doubt that." But if she had not come peacefully, would he not have heard her struggle? Nausea ate away at him. *Dear God, what is going on?* "Please, just tell me what you want. Why are you tormenting us?"

"If you must know, I heard your wife had family in town. I was just stopping by because I had forgotten to deliver this note—" he pulled an envelope out of his shirt pocket, "—and then I found you out here."

Matthew snatched the note from Eric's hand and tore it

open. He could not believe his eyes. "You want money for Aimee. You want me to *buy* my wife, like she is some common prostitute."

"Your words, not mine. I am in need of some ransom money."

"A ransom implies that she is with you against her will, and yet you insist that she is with you by her choice. Allow me to see that my wife is safe, and then I will be able to pay." Matthew cringed when he saw the sum of money on the page. He did not even have half of it. Obviously, Eric was taking advantage of the fact that her family was near.

"You are hardly in a position to make demands of me. I said your wife is safe now, but that can change. I was never truly attached to her. She is quite annoying. If you were smart, you would have separated from her weeks ago." Honeysett brushed at some dirt on his trousers.

Matthew knew the blasted man was trying to rile him up, but it was working. "Just…give me the day to gather the money. Where can I find you?"

A satisfied smile twisted Honeysett's face. "Our inn's address is on the bottom of the note. And don't plan on going there to make some heroic attempt. I know people there, so you have no chance of finding her, and it's not exactly…your kind of place to frequent, preacher."

If this man was hiding Matthew's wife in a brothel, Matthew did not know what he would do to the miscreant.

Light pooled from the window of the cabin. One of Aimee's brothers was up. Matthew would never be able to explain the situation to them. They would declare Matthew was an unfit husband if Aimee had been snatched from their bed while he was sleeping and was now held at ransom. No, Eric Honeysett was Matthew's problem, and he would handle this alone.

"Go, Honeysett. You will get your money. Just do not harm my wife."

"I expect the full sum by midnight tomorrow. After that, I will not be able to tolerate her any longer, and I can't make promises on what happens to her."

Matthew internalized a groan. "Get off of my property, Honeysett."

"Very well. Good luck getting those funds without her family involved." Matthew cringed as the man's laughter filled the darkness. Soon, he was gone. Mathew couldn't help but wonder what treatment Aimee would receive when Honeysett returned to her. He could contact the constable, but that could be too tricky, and Aimee's family would hear about it then. Matthew may have until midnight the next day, but it would be better for everyone involved if he could get the money as soon as he could.

"What are you doing out here?"

Matthew nearly jumped out of his skin.

"Relax, it's just me. Calm down, man."

"Sebastien. What are you doing out here?" A sigh escaped Matthew.

"I already asked you the same."

"I was just…getting some fresh air." Matthew ran a hand through his hair, which he only just now realized was damp with a cold sweat.

"It's the middle of the night, man." Sebastien shook his head. "I tell you what, Matthew." He glanced behind him. "I know the rest of my family is a little unsure, but I believe that you are a good match for our little Aimee. She loves you more than anyone she has ever been with."

Matthew wanted to crawl out of his skin. This would

be comforting to hear…any other time. But he hated to be reminded that his wife who once hated him but now loved him was probably being tortured at this moment. There was no way Sebastien could learn about this. It was Matthew's problem to solve.

"Look, I will try to talk to them about you. They tend to laugh me off, as the middle child who has always been trying to settle disputes, but I know they will listen to me in time. We will leave you two alone soon enough. I know you are taking care of her."

I know you are taking care of her. A scream built up inside Matthew's chest as he followed Sebastien into the house.

Chapter 20

❧

A thousand rocks were pounding against Aimee's head at once. Her eyelids were too heavy to lift. Nausea overwhelmed her stomach, forcing her to sit up. She only rose a few inches from the bed before thick rope cut into her wrists and her ankles. Panic seized her breath. Finally, her eyes had the will to open as pain shot through her muscles. She was not on the ship. She was not at home.

It took her eyes several moments to adjust to the darkness as she tried to recognize her surroundings. All she could make out was the bedpost at her feet. Her wrists were bound together, and then tied behind her to the headboard. Her feet were bound similarly.

What on earth had happened? She had no memory of how she got here. "H-hello?" Her throat was dry. Just a simple word was difficult to produce. "Matthew?" The room was filled with a foul, musty aroma. Rowdy voices ascended from below, instantly reminding her of life on board a ship with sailors. Aimee felt the urge to cry, but she knew that would get her nowhere. At least she could feel that she was on land. It was comforting to know that wherever she was, she was not travelling farther and farther away from home. Her heart sank. It was good that she was not moving farther away from Matthew.

A creaking noise rent the air, right outside her door. A footstep on a floorboard. Next, she heard the rattle of keys. Adrenaline pumped through her body as the door slowly opened. Light poured in the room, temporarily rendering Aimee sightless. She blinked frantically, but every sliver of light that entered her vision felt like a shard of glass stabbing her head. Nausea hit her stomach once again. She forced herself to take a calm breath as she pried her eyes open once more.

Eric Honeysett grinned down at her, the light from the doorway behind illuminating his tall frame. "Well, the sleeping beauty has awoken. Here, I thought I had a few more hours to kill before I returned to you. The medicine man had assured me that his concoction would work all through the night. Oh, you poor dear, you must have been so frightened to wake up all alone in this manner." His tone dripped with condescending sweetness.

"Eric Honeysett, you will unfasten me immediately and take me home to Matthew." Aimee lifted her chin in false confidence.

"Oh, the plucky little woman demands something of me? How presumptuous." He chuckled, sauntering closer to the bed. "I had half a mind to tie something around your blasted mouth so I would not have to hear your complaints, but I thought you might be willing to cooperate. I told that man you were feisty, and he insisted you would be quiet for several hours. I should go demand my money back."

Whatever substance he had used to induce her sleep had worked, however. Her mind was still foggy, and her joints ached. "If you do not let me go immediately, I will scream!"

This time, he threw his head back in laughter. "My darling Mrs. Emery, I do regret to inform you that you are inside an inn, right above a tavern. I assure you, the sound of a woman's scream is nothing out of the ordinary here. In fact, passersby might simply be amused. So please, do go ahead and scream. I would not care."

Aimee's hands balled up into fists. If only she were free, she would kick this monster of a man with all of her might and scratch the skin off of his face. She tried to work against the bindings, but that just seemed to make them tighter and more painful. It felt like her wrists was bleeding, but she wasn't quite sure. She couldn't feel her fingers, and her toes were on the way to becoming numb as well.

"Please, Mr. Honeysett, the least you can do is tell me what you want from me. I had thought you were well on your way back home. Matthew saw you board the ship himself." Her throat was so dry that her voice cracked with every word.

"Well, *milady*, I was in fact on a ship back to the Caribbean, when I received word you had some family in town. I could not waste the opportunity to *get to know* them better." He lit a match, illuminating the room, before he used it to ignite a single candle.

"Have you done something awful to my brothers? To Matthew? Just tell me what you want." Tears threatened to form in her scratchy eyes, but she blinked them back.

"I have not harmed anyone, my dear Mrs. Emery. There is no need to worry. And if your husband does as I ask, no one will be harmed." He sat on the edge of the bed beside her. With him this close she could smell the rum on his breath. The foul odor made her want to shrink away, but her bindings prohibited any movement.

"What do you want from Matthew? You know we have nothing. If it's me you want, you would have tried a lot harder to be a gentleman when we were back on the ship. And certainly you know that kidnapping a lady is not the way to win her affections."

"Aimee, I have no need to win your affections, when I can just as easily win your fortune."

Aimee gritted her teeth. Of course this was about her money. She should have easily guessed that. "What do you want with my money, Honeysett? I recall you telling me you had quite a fortune yourself."

"Oh, it is quite a long story, my pet. You needn't be bothered with it."

"I beg you, Eric, tell me. I don't think you have anywhere else to be, do you?" She offered him her sweetest look, the one she reserved for only the most elite socialites back in London. If she got him to talk to her long enough, maybe she could think of a way out of here.

His expression softened for a moment. Was he taking pity on her? Rethinking his actions? "I suppose it won't hurt to tell you about my life. You're just a silly, little girl."

Aimee ignored his dig at her intelligence and offered him another sweet smile. "Eric, please. These bonds are hurting me. You know I, too, have nowhere to go. I haven't even an idea where we are. Could you please loosen them?"

Eric stared at her for several moments. He jumped up, locked the door, and returned to her side. "All right. But if you make any stupid attempts to escape, know that I am not bound to any promises. I will not hesitate to hurt you. It would be a shame if you returned to your precious Captain Emery…in less than pristine condition. We all know the righteous preacher would probably reject used goods." His hand reached out and slowly slid down the length of her side.

Panic tore at Aimee's stomach. This man had already attempted this on her, so she knew he had it in him. She would have to tread carefully around him. Besides, it was true that she had no idea where she was or anything of the sort. But that didn't mean it would stop her from making an attempt to escape the moment he turned his back.

Ever so slowly, he pulled a blade from his belt and held it up to the light. He brought it close to her neck as if reminding her that he had the power to kill her, before he grabbed her ankles and lifted her skirt well past the line of decency. If only her feet were free already and he did not have a weapon, she would have kicked him in the face. He sliced the rope that bound her. Quickly, he moved up to her wrists and freed them, as well. It felt like every nerve in her hands and feet were being stabbed with needles as the blood rushed back to them. She tried rubbing her wrists and her ankles, but nothing quite helped the pain.

"I do beg your pardon if they hurt you. My intention was to render you motionless, my dear, not to inflict pain."

Aimee rolled her eyes. The man was an idiot if he thought she believed that. "Please tell me, Eric. Why do you need my family's money if you are the wealthy man you claim to be?"

"Well, Aimee, I am afraid I have not been completely honest with you." Eric nudged her over and sat next to her on the bed. Aimee backed away to the other edge, determined to maintain a safe distance from him. "As you well know, my father was a wealthy owner of a plantation. When he died, I made certain he left the plantation to me, as I was his only child.

"I did not get along well with the slaves there, especially since I was the illegitimate child of one of them. Nobody quite understood that *I* had power over *them*. Notwithstanding all of that, I did not enjoy life on the plantation. I loved the money and the comfortable living, but I did not enjoy the business work." Aimee was shocked the man was confessing this to her. He truly was not the wealthy gentleman of fine breeding she had first thought he was. "My mind is not cut out for numbers, you see. They are beneath me. So I sold the plantation and lived off the money for a while. But I do like to spend, and some unfortunate gambling activities took away much of my funds. So now, I go from place to place and make most of my earnings by…well, by not exactly *honest* means. But it gets me what I want, and I eat the finest foods and purchase the best clothes. I'm living just fine this way, but I could use the extra funds I will be getting from your family soon."

Aimee wondered how her family was reacting. Her father would probably give the money to get her back, and she would be safe in no time. However, they would be unhappy with Matthew, as she had gone missing under his watch. Aimee tried to grasp a memory as to how Eric had gotten her out of the bedroom, where she had been right next to Mathew, but her mind was still far too foggy. If only she could just keep Eric talking until he was distracted enough for her to make an attempt to escape this wretched place. If she were able to leave on her own, then her family would never have to pay what this lunatic demanded.

* * *

Matthew barely had a cent to his name, but he gathered everything he had. He prayed that there was some kindness residing in Mr. Honeysett's heart, and he would let Aimee go with all that Matthew could gather. This was his responsibility, and he could not bring himself to bother Aimee's family with the manner.

Matthew squinted at the address Mr. Honeysett had given him. He prayed this place would be easy to locate. All he wanted was to see his wife.

How was Aimee faring through all of this? Matthew knew she was a strong woman, but there was only so much a person could take. After all, she had nearly been the victim of a horrible abduction not that long ago, besides everything they had endured with Honeysett in the past. *Please, dear God, let Aimee be all right. Do not allow Honeysett to harm her.*

Chapter 21

Sebastien waited until his brothers and father were outside before he bounded back indoors to check Matthew's desk. He doubted Matthew's claim that Aimee had arisen early to visit some friends in town. Something was amiss. It was unlike Aimee to leave without saying goodbye or eating breakfast, and Matthew was acting far too worried for a man whose wife was out on social visits. Something was wrong, and he was determined to find out what was happening to his sister.

He had been polite enough to not question Matthew about the envelope that was in his hand when he had found him outdoors at night. But now it was time to see for himself what the mysterious note contained. After a short moment of rifling through the drawers, he located the dark, sprawling handwriting he had seen the night before. It was addressed to Mr. Matthew Emery and the Dawson family. Hmm.

He tore the letter out of the envelope and the breath *wooshed* from his body as he read its contents. Aimee was gone? And who was this Eric Honeysett fellow? And how on earth was Matthew planning on getting that amount of money all on his own? Back in London, he knew that Matthew had never been able to earn enough money on his own to maintain a steady living. Surely he did not make enough as the reverend of a small colony's church here to pay off this ransom. The man clearly needed help, and he was too afraid to ask for it. Sebastien would have to find a way to get his brothers to help Aimee without embarrassing Matthew.

* * *

Matthew cringed as he approached the address Mr. Honeysett had given him. Just as he had suspected, it was not a reputable location. He prayed Aimee was safe and unharmed upstairs.

As soon as he entered the building, the fumes of alcohol and rotting food assaulted his senses. The place was not overly crowded, as it was the middle of the day, but Matthew feared what this tavern was like at night. Hopefully Aimee stayed far away from the commotion. He could not help but remember the last time he had been in a tavern with Aimee.

A barmaid approached him, her gait quick and flighty. Obviously, she was happy to have a customer. "What can I get for ya, sir?" She tossed her braid over her shoulder, trying to draw his attention there.

Matthew kept his gaze steady. "I was told I could find Mr. Eric Honeysett here. May I speak to him?"

Her green eyes darkened. She looked to the side. "He said he was expectin' someone. May I get your name, sir?"

"Matthew Emery."

"I'll go tell him you're here." She scurried off upstairs, her skirts flouncing with each step she took.

Matthew leaned against the bar counter, dread tainting his every breath. This would probably not work, but he prayed there was some kindness in the man's heart. Surely no one was entirely evil.

After several moments, the young lady returned with Mr. Honeysett trailing behind. She floated over to stand behind the bar and suddenly seemed completely interested in cleaning the counter.

Eric cleared the final stair and crossed his arms across his chest as he approached Matthew. "So soon, Mr. Emery? I did not expect my letter to be fulfilled *this* quickly."

"Mr. Honeysett, I beg you to listen to me." Matthew pulled the money he had amassed in the last hours and offered it to the man.

Mr. Honeysett glanced at the sum, threw his head back, and laughed. "This is barely half of what I demanded. Do you think this is a time for bargaining? I told you what I require."

The barmaid stopped her cleaning and stared at Honeysett. He caught her gaze and shook his head sharply. She scurried away.

"Please, Mr. Honeysett, this is my wife we are talking about. Take the money and be on your way, just give me my wife."

"You cannot just disregard our agreement, Emery. This is not a business deal. I am not here to bargain with you. Go home and get the money, or never see your wife again. It's that simple."

"Honeysett, let me buy you a drink, and we can have a discussion. Please."

Chapter 22

꧁꧂

Aimee had no idea why Eric had been called away in such a rush, but she was certainly happy he had. In his haste, he had forgotten to retie her bindings. Her happiness was cut short, however, when she realized the door was locked from the outside. She exhaled, searching around the room for another way out. Some light seeped in through the window drapes, signifying dawn was already well past her.

The window. Aimee had a way out. She threw the curtains to the side, dismayed to see she was on the second floor of a building, looking out over a filthy alleyway. It still gave her no clue as to where she was, and she was not sure she could make it all the way down to the street. Could she have perhaps been taken to another town? Oh, she would be terrified if she got out and could not find her way home. Surely Matthew had noticed she was missing by this point. Was he on his way to save her? Had he gotten whatever sum Honeysett had demanded? Well, there was no time to wait for her husband to come and save her. Honeysett could be back any moment now.

From her days in London, Aimee could remember her best friend, Eden, telling her tales of climbing out of her bedroom window to play with her brother. Eden's room had also been on the second floor, but she had the convenience of a tree right next to it. All she had to do was hop out and climb down the footing the tree offered. Aimee peered below once more. No such luck for her. There was not a tree in sight along the alleyway. If only she had a rope to propel her down or something.

Aimee raced back to the bed. The lengths of rope Honeysett had used to bind her were all severed in half, so they would not do her much good. But if she tied them together, perhaps they would at least make her jump that much shorter. Aimee make quick work of the ropes, tying them in the knots she had seen sailors use. Hopefully they wouldn't break, but right now, Aimee did not have many other options.

Just as she forced the window open, the door burst open and light poured in from behind her. Aimee froze in shock. Mr. Honeysett would kill her. Nausea welled up in her stomach to the point that her shoulders sagged and she feared she would bend over and cast up her accounts. She waited for his hand to grip her shoulder, his sharp voice to rent the air. But nothing happened.

"Miss?"

Aimee swung around, shocked to hear the voice of a female. A small woman clad in a cheap, low-cut gown gazed at her shyly, her large, green eyes blinking.

"Ummm…hello." Aimee dropped the rope from her hands. The nausea in her stomach seemed to settle down, even though she still knew she was not safe. No doubt this woman would report back to Honeysett the second she left.

"I…I came to help ya, miss, but it seems to me yer doing a fine job on yer own." A smile lurked at the corner of her mouth as she shut the door behind her.

"You wanted to help me? Why?"

"I've heard of that terrible Honeysett man, and from the small interactions I've had with him, I know he treats women horribly. I heard that he stole ya from yer husband?"

"Yes, that's true."

"Well, I'd like to help ya. Now, just where were ya planning on going after ya climbed out that window?" The woman stepped nearer once again.

"I…I was going to find my husband."

"He is downstairs, miss."

"I must go to him!" Aimee's spirits lifted. Matthew had come for her!

"No, miss, that's not a great idea. Mr. Honeysett is downstairs talkin' to him right now. I don't suggest ya go home, either. The moment Honeysett notices yer gone, he'll assume that's where ya went."

"W-where do you suggest I go then?" Aimee eyed the woman suspiciously. Had Honeysett sent her to trap Aimee? She had no reason to trust this woman.

"Ah, I can see ya aren't too sure about me, miss. But I hate to say, yer other options don't look too great, either. Let me help ya. I once was with a man like Honeysett, and I don't want another woman to be hurt like I was. Please. Come with me."

What did Aimee have to lose? After all, she did not even know if she'd be able to find her way home alone. She nodded.

"Oh, excellent, miss. My name's Cecily, by the way."

Aimee smiled back at Cecily. "Aimee Emery. Nice to meet

you."

"Now, follow me. We must hurry. Honeysett will never think to look for you right under his nose." She grabbed Aimee's hand and pulled her out of the room, her gait light and upbeat. Aimee struggled to follow at her quick pace.

"Where are we going?"

"Shh!" Cecily giggled. "My room." They climbed up a flight of stairs and stopped halfway down the hall.

The room was surprisingly bright and clean for the building they were in. The walls were painted yellow, and flowers adorned the windowsill and the small desk in the corner of the room. "This is quite lovely," Aimee whispered. It reminded her of her room back home in London, although much smaller and less richly decorated.

"Well, thank ya, Mrs. Emery. I try to keep it as pleasant as possible. I hate it downstairs, and I like to forget that where I live is part of the same building as where I work."

"Thank you for your help, Cecily. I don't deserve it."

"It's the right thing to do. I may work in a place like this, but that doesn't mean I don't remember the Bible passages my mama taught me."

Aimee watched as the girl tidied up some papers and hair brushes that were scattered around the room. "Well, miss. I'd better get back downstairs. Mr. Honeysett will notice yer missing soon, and we don't need him suspecting me. Then he'd find ya out for sure."

"You're probably right." Aimee glanced out the window. It was on the other side of the building and offered a view of the street below.

"I'll let ya know what's going on downstairs as soon as I can. Yer husband looked worried down there."

Aimee swallowed. She prayed Honeysett wouldn't hurt Matthew.

"I'll be back before ya know it." Cecily moved toward the door. "Your husband is a good man, Mrs. Emery. He loves you very much."

* * *

Matthew could not stop his feet from dragging on the walk back to his home. His trip had been unsuccessful, and now he had to face his fears and speak to Aimee's family. They would not be happy with him, but at least they would have the funds to set Aimee free.

He hated that he had been so close to her and unable to save her, but he knew any risky movements would capture the horrid man's attention and threaten her well-being. No, this time he would have to do what Honeysett demanded, or he feared Aimee would have to deal with the consequences of his failures.

"Matthew!"

He knew that voice. Oh, how he dreaded to turn around and face Aimee's family.

"Matthew! Why didn't you tell us? We can help you!" Sebastien quickened his pace and met Matthew halfway on the block. "We can help Aimee." He paused a moment to catch his breath. "Do you know where in the tavern he is keeping her?"

"How did you find out?" was all Matthew could bring himself

to say.

"I knew something was wrong. You were acting strangely, and Aimee was gone. Then I remembered the envelope I had seen you holding. I found it in your desk. We can help you, Matthew, and I don't think we even need to give him our money. Between you and my brothers, we far outnumber the man. We can get Aimee home safely and see him sent straight to jail for his actions."

"Sebastien, I don't think you understand the threat of this man. He is a snake. I don't know how well guarded he has her, but it is not safe just to barge in and demand her to be released."

"Well, then we pay him. Goodness knows, we can afford it."

"Are you certain?"

"Anything for my favorite little sister. Come on. Let's go back and get my brothers to use as reinforcement." Sebastien laughed and offered Matthew his hand to shake, and for the first time in his life, Matthew felt like part of a family.

Chapter 23

E ric Honeysett felt the need to kill someone. Preferably someone with the last name of Emery. Honestly, at this point, he didn't care whether it was Aimee or Matthew. The blasted little man had stolen her away while he was speaking with him! How preposterous. Eric felt cheated. He had thought the preacher was an honest man, but he supposed he was like any other preacher he had met. A hypocrite.

The voice of reason inside Eric's head told him to wait, to let it be. There was no reason to keep bothering the family. They were free of him. But Eric's pride would not allow that. No, they had wronged him, and he would not let that slide by. No doubt the woman was well on her way back to their home at the moment. Well, Eric knew where they lived, and he could easily abduct her once again. He would teach them they had upset the wrong man.

Eric slammed his fist against the bed post. He had no idea how the couple had planned it, but he could tell from the bits of rope that were tied together on the floor and the open window that the stupid girl had climbed down while Matthew had distracted him. Eric was not typically a man prone to violence, but he felt the sudden urge to beat the fiery spirit out of the girl. Eric's father had taught him that when he wanted something, he should demand it and get anyone who tried to stop him out of his way. Oh, when he got his hands on her...not to mention her stupid, annoying husband.

Eric slammed the door behind him, feeling a small amount of satisfaction as the wall shook with his power. In his haste, he almost ran into the little barmaid, Cecily. "Oh...forgive me," he muttered.

"Where are ya off to in such a hurry, Mr. Honeysett?" She backed away from him.

"That blasted girl has run off. I must find her. I think her husband helped her when she was here. He...he served as some sort of diversion" Eric hated to admit he had failed, but obviously he had fallen trap to their schemes. There was no denying it.

"I'm sorry, sir. Is there anything I can do to help ya?" She batted her eyelashes at him.

"I don't think there's anything you can do, unless you saw her leave. I need to know if she's alone or if she's with her husband."

"I didn't see her, Mr. Honeysett. I was in back while you were talking to the man, checking my stocks for the night and getting some food ready for the girls upstairs."

Of course she was. Eric imagined Aimee was getting farther and farther away with each moment he spoke to the barmaid. "Well, let me know if you hear anything. Perhaps one of the ladies upstairs noticed something was off. Here's for your troubles." He tossed her a coin as he passed her in the hallway and left the building.

Now, he did have to acknowledge that Aimee was smarter than most people gave her credit for. Perhaps she would not go straight home. No, she would go somewhere else, somewhere nearby…somewhere she felt safe. Ah, the little mouse was probably hiding inside her husband's church.

* * *

The waiting was killing Aimee, but she was just happy that she was away from Eric at the moment. Besides, it was nice to be with Cecily. The girl was fun to chat with, and Aimee owed her life to her. She would have to ask her papa to give the girl some money for her troubles. Maybe she would be able to live somewhere other than this horrible tavern if she could afford another life.

Cecily paused in her cleaning and looked at Aimee. "Tell me about yer husband, Mrs. Emery. I do dislike the silence."

"You were correct when you said he is a fine man, Cecily. He would do anything for me. I love him very much. We ended up together against all odds, because we hated each other back home in London. I was a rather snobbish girl there, going to every ball held in town. I was raised quite comfortably, as I held the title of lady and my father was wealthy."

Cecily grinned, her eyes wide, as Aimee spoke.

"Matthew, on the other hand, showed up on our church's doorsteps one morning when he was just a child, and he was raised by our reverend. He got into shipping and sailing, but he became a reverend himself soon enough. That's what we are doing in town. He has a church here that he was called to preach at, and he seems to enjoy it here. I won't miss London too much if we stay here. Well, after I get out of this mess."

"Why did ya leave London, Mrs. Emery? And how did ya end up falling in love with him if ya didn't like each other at first?" Cecily finally ceased her cleaning and sat down on the bed next to Aimee.

"Well, my best friend, Eden, had run away from home—for good reasons. My other friend, Ivy, and I decided we needed to find her to see that she was safe. And then one day, I was angry with Matthew, so I stole away from him in the city of Port Royal. A man from an…establishment similar to this caught me and was trying to auction me off to the men there. Matthew found me and insisted they could not sell me, as I was his fiancé. That was a lie, but he did it to save me. The men joked they would let me go if he proved it by marrying me right then and there. They didn't expect us to actually do it, but suddenly…we were married. I expected us to separate at the best opportunity possible and forget it ever happened, but Matthew stood by the promise he made that day. He insisted we make our marriage work, and eventually…it did. And I could not be happier, honestly."

"I'm glad yer happy, Mrs. Emery. I'm just sorry yer in a mess with this horrible Mr. Honeysett. He is not a pleasant man. I can just imagine the pain both you and your husband are in to be separated from each other over this, especially after all it sounds like ya have been through." Cecily rose once more and picked up her feather duster.

"Thank you so much for your help with this, Cecily. Honestly, I cannot express to you how grateful I am for your help. I owe you my life. Is there any way I can repay you for your kindness?" Aimee leaned back against Cecily's pillow as she ate the chunk of bread and cheese she had brought her.

"Nah, Mrs. Emery. Ya don't owe me a thing." The girl waved the duster around the room, cleaning bits that Aimee was certain were already quite clean. She had noticed Cecily hated to be still.

"Please, call me Aimee."

Cecily peeked up at her with a smile, her eyes bright green against her dark lashes. "Aimee. Ya know, there is one thing."

"What's that? Anything." Suddenly interested, Aimee sat up from the edge of the bed.

"Well, Aimee. I'm not sure how ya are going to feel about this, but…Oh, never mind. It's silly." She continued her dusting.

Aimee stilled the girl's hand. "Please, tell me."

"Well…I have always wanted to…that is, I was wondering if yer husband would mind if I tried coming to his church one week?" Her meek smile was so endearing that Aimee wanted to pull her into her arms and hug her. "That is, I understand if ya say no. I would understand if he doesn't want a…someone like me in his church. That would make sense, really."

Aimee's emotions hit her so hard that she nearly began to cry. The fact that this girl was struggling this much just because she thought she would not be accepted in a church was heartbreaking. "Cecily, of course we would love to have you come to church with us. We would be honored to see you there. Consider yourself my guest. You can sit next to me, and then you can join us for lunch after at my home. I could not be any happier, my dear."

"Oh, thank you so much!" Cecily hugged her. "Ya know, I

have never met a real lady before. I am so glad that you are just as good and kind as I always imagined one would be."

Aimee smiled at the irony of the girl's statement. "You are not missing a lot, Cecily. I can assure you that if you met me a few months ago when I was a lady in London, you would not have liked me. I doubt I would have even spoken to you then. I used to be so petty. I regret it. And most of London is just like I used to act."

"Well, that's quite all right, Aimee. I am just glad that I do know ya now."

Aimee sighed. "I do hate the waiting, though."

"I know. But I want to make sure Mr. Honeysett is back here before ya leave. I don't want ya to cross paths, especially if ya would be alone." Cecily patted her on the back.

"But it is going to be dark out soon. I hope I can leave before it gets too late."

"I'm sure all will be well."

"Cecily!" Aimee jumped at the sound of Honeysett's voice in the distance. What if he came in the room?

Cecily caught her gaze. "Not to worry. His voice is coming from the floor below us. He doesn't know which room is mine. He won't get ahold of ya if I go out there now. But I suppose it's yer time to go now, isn't it?"

Panic filled Aimee at the realization. "Yes, I suppose it is." Aimee did not care about how she knew a lady like her should or should not behave. She pulled the girl into her arms and embraced her. "Thank you again for your help. I will see you in church on Sunday, Cecily."

"Thank you. Now leave the moment you hear I'm down-stairs!"

Cecily shut the door behind her and Aimee listened as her

footsteps faded. Eric's voice boomed in the distance, but she couldn't quite make out what he was saying. Nonetheless, it sounded like he was a good distance away from the staircase. Adrenaline rushed through her. This was her moment. *Oh God, please don't let him see me.* Cecily had explained to Aimee how to find the rear exit to the building without being seen. She just prayed this would work.

Aimee tried to keep the door as silent as she could as it closed behind her. Still, its sound scared her half to death. She tip-toed down the long hallway to the stairwell. Luckily, no one else was outside their rooms to see her leave. Eric would probably interrogate all of the women in this building to discover if they had seen her leave.

Finally, she made it to the staircase. Each step she made sounded magnified in her ears, but she was certain it was only her imagination. She made it down one flight of stairs. Two more to go, then she would see the door that Cecily had detailed to her. Once she got through that and found the kitchen, she would see the back door and freedom.

"The blasted woman is not in her home. I checked thoroughly, as no one was home at the time."

Aimee froze. It sounded like Eric was directly below her. Was he coming closer, or walking away? Tears filled Aimee's eyes, and for a moment, she felt as if she could not move. Soon, however, his voice faded away. Strength returned to her body once more, and she ran the rest of the way down the stairs. Immediately, she spotted the door Cecily had described. Without a second glance, Aimee bounded through it, past the kitchen, and straight out the back door. The wretched air of the alleyway had never smelled sweeter than it did to Aimee at that moment.

Chapter 23

Cecily had given her brief directions on how to get back to her home, and Aimee was determined to find it without running into any trouble. She would have to hurry, as night was falling fast.

Chapter 24

A imee had never been happier to see her tiny house in her entire life. All the lights were off when she approached it, so she made quick work of lighting some lanterns. It had grown bitterly dark outside. But where was her family? Was no one waiting for her?

"Matthew! Sebastien! Where is everyone?" A lot of the contents of her home were strewn about the room. Panic filled Aimee. She knew Eric had been here, but had he harmed anyone? *Oh, no. Oh, dear God, no.*

There was not a single person home. Hot tears filled Aimee's eyes. Had they returned to find her, and was Eric bothering them now? Oh, she hated to return to that awful tavern, but she feared she may have to. However, there was something she must do first.

Aimee stormed outside and down the street to the constable's house. The man attended their church, and Aimee hoped he would hear her out. She hoped he knew some other men who would be able to help her stop Mr. Honeysett.

She knocked on the door, although she figured it was well past visiting hours. A dog barked from inside. Seconds seemed to tick by, and yet no one came to the door. Perhaps the constable was asleep? Or, or maybe he had not heard her knock. Just as she raised her hand to knock again, the door opened.

"Mrs. Emery." The kindly middle-aged man opened the door wider and motioned for her to come inside. "Do come in. The air has grown quite chilly." Aimee allowed him to escort her inside. "Now, my dear, what brings you to my house at this time of night? Is something wrong?"

"Oh, everything is wrong, Mr. Lewis. I'm not even sure where to begin."

"Where is your husband, Mrs. Emery?" He grabbed a shawl that was hanging on the coat rack and offered it to her. Aimee gladly took it. Cecily had given her a dress to wear, as she had been in her nightgown when Mr. Honeysett had abducted her. However, it was still cold. She had not been thinking about the chill in the air when she had run from her house.

"Well, that is part of the problem. And it's a long problem, but I pray you will listen to me. Mr. Lewis."

"Of course, milady. That is my job, after all."

Aimee detailed to the man what had happened to her, beginning with what had happened last night and finishing with her rushed visit to his home. Thankfully, he seemed to believe her.

"Well, I suppose we have to go arrest this man. He has done unthinkable things. Where can we find him?"

"I don't know the name or the address of the tavern, but I found my way back here, so I am certain I can find the tavern again. Please understand he is a dangerous man."

Mr. Lewis nodded. "Just give me a moment, Mrs. Emery, and we will be on our way."

"Oh, I cannot thank you enough, Mr. Lewis."

"You and your husband are good people, Mrs. Emery. I am happy to help you."

* * *

Matthew was certain his blood must be boiling as he met with Mr. Honeysett and Aimee's family. Aimee's brothers insisted that Mr. Honeysett allow them to see her first before they gave him the money, and the man insisted that he had not seen her since the morning.

"If you haven't seen her, then where were you keeping her?" Matthew clenched his fists in an attempt to keep their encounter violence-free.

"I don't know what game you are playing, Emery, but you can go look for yourself. I was keeping her upstairs, and now she is gone. I know she went with you, so you can give up the ruse. What do you want with me?"

Sebastien stepped forward. "Mr. Honeysett, you stated that if we gave you the money, you would return Aimee to us. We have the money. Now show us our sister. It's quite simple. Show us the room where she was, if you insist she is gone."

"Very well!" Honeysett threw his hands in the air.

Matthew didn't know what to believe. Had Aimee escaped? Did Mr. Honeysett truly not know where she was? Was she out wandering the streets somewhere alone? Or, had Mr. Honeysett done something terrible to her? The uncertainty of it all terrified Matthew.

He followed Mr. Honeysett up the stairs, still appalled that the man had kept his wife in a disreputable place like this. It brought back awful memories of Matthew's first years. No one deserved to be exposed to a life like that, especially not sweet Aimee.

After they travelled up one flight of stairs, Mr. Honeysett stopped at a door. "This is where she was. I found some ropes tied together, and the window was open, so I assumed she jumped out while you were here to distract me. She disappeared in the time that I was speaking to you. I assumed it was all part of your plan."

Matthew wasn't certain if he wanted to punch something, cheer, or vomit. It did sound like Aimee had made it out of here on her own. However, she should have been home a long time ago, and no one had seen her coming or going. *Oh no.* Was it possible that she had escaped only to get lost somewhere on the streets, terrified and alone? Or worse yet, had she been picked up by some unsavory sorts? *No, no, no.*

"Are you telling us the truth?" Anton's voice boomed from the entryway. He stepped closer, his frame imposing. Honeysett was surrounded by men just as large as him. Was there a way they could capture him together and take him to the authorities for his actions? And even then, would they ever find Aimee again?

"Yes, I am telling you the truth. What would I get out of the wench going missing? I asked for ransom money, and I doubt I am going to get it at this point. I have nothing to gain from her being missing, and you know that well."

"They are right this way, mister." Matthew recognized the barmaid's voice and soon saw her at the entry to the door.

What was she doing upstairs? The bar had been quite busy when they had arrived. He was surprised she was able to spend a moment away from it.

The barmaid bounded into the room, followed by...Mr. Lewis? Matthew recognized the constable immediately. Well, that was perfect timing. They were in need of a constable.

"Matthew!" A shock of blond curls stole Matthew's breath with surprise as Aimee charged into the crowded room and straight into his arms. Matthew pulled her tighter against him. He was afraid he would never let her go. He had no idea what she was doing here or how she had gotten here, but Matthew had never been happier to see the little spitfire in his life.

"Mr. Eric Honeysett, I am Mr. Lewis, the constable of this town. You are under arrest and will be coming with me immediately."

Honeysett's eyes opened large, revealing his inner panic as he frantically searched the room. First he looked at the number of people blocking his exit, then at Aimee, and then to the window.

"He's going to jump!" Matthew cried, but Honeysett was already half out the window. Although it was a long drop, Matthew assumed the man would still be able to run after he hit the ground. "Get him!" Aimee's brothers and the constable rushed out to find the man.

Aimee lurched forward to join them, but Matthew held her fast in his arms. "You have done enough, sweet lady. Let them handle it for once." He let her lean her head against his chest and appreciated the feel of her in the crook of his neck. "I am a blessed man, Aimee. I was afraid I would never see you again."

She smiled. "God has a funny way of always tossing us back together, doesn't He?"

Matthew chuckled. "That He does, my dear."

"Got him!" A man's voice rang out from the alleyway below. Matthew ushered Aimee to the window, where, to his relief, he saw Mr. Honeysett bound up. "The fool broke his leg in the fall. But I am sure we can patch it up," Mr. Lewis shouted.

"Thank you, constable." Matthew squeezed Aimee closer. "I guess it's time to get out of this wretched place, isn't it?"

Aimee nodded. "Let's get home."

Chapter 25

I t felt wonderful to be back in their church once more. Aimee's heart fluttered when she looked up at her husband, preaching at the pulpit. Her family had bid her adieu once they had seen how much Aimee and Matthew had proved they cared for each other. They promised to send a little money each year as a kind of dowry, and to ensure they could live comfortably. Aimee appreciated the gesture, but she was certain they would not need the extra funds. Whatever they received, they would probably donate to someone who needed it more desperately.

Aimee shared a smile with Cecily, who sat in the pew beside to her. It warmed Aimee's soul to know that at least her troubles with Eric seemed to have made another person's life a lot brighter in the end. The girl seemed to be enjoying the sermon. *Father, you really do work in mysterious ways.*

After the service, Cecily joined Aimee and Matthew at home for a meal. Aimee appreciated the chance to get to know the young woman better. Goodness, she hoped that the girl's life would get brighter with her weekly visits. Maybe one day she would be able to leave the tavern where she worked.

After they escorted the girl back to the tavern, Matthew threw his arm around Aimee. "I am still glad you are safe, darling."

She smiled up at him. "I am glad *you* are safe, too."

"Do you think our adventures are over now? I cannot imagine something else popping up." He tugged her a little closer.

"I hope they are…but only for a while. I do think I might grow to miss our days at sea after some time here. I'm not sure how I used to tolerate my static life in London."

"As much as I enjoy it here, I think I will grow tired of this life as well. But I have been meaning to tell you, I received a letter yesterday from Reverend Melville. He is recovering quite well, and he expressed some interest in returning to his congregation in a few months. Only if we wanted him to, of course."

Aimee paused her step. "Matthew, that is wonderful!"

He grinned. "You think so?"

"Yes, I do."

"I am glad, dear. I was hoping I would be able to pick up the *Cross's Victory* again and turn her into a missionary ship. We would need to find a crew who was willing to join us in our endeavors, but I think it is possible, with what money we do have."

Aimee gasped. "I think that is an excellent idea, Matthew!"

"And who knows. Maybe we will see your friends during our travels. I know how you miss them."

"I love that idea, Matthew." Aimee leaned her head against his shoulder as they continued on their walk home. They had no idea what adventures awaited them, but Aimee knew she could handle them if she had Matthew by her side through it all.

Epilogue

Near Kingston, Jamaica
1698

Aimee set her broom aside to brace a hand against her lower back. It was getting more and more difficult to do simple housework. She smoothed her hand over her swelling stomach. The baby kicked. Aimee leaned against the wall of the new little home Matthew had built for them and smiled.

"How are you doing, my princess?" Her husband's quiet voice drifted closer from where she had left him in his study. He entered the room, his expression playful. His blond hair was tousled and his blue eyes shown bright with excitement. He must have been writing a sermon. "Were you doing housework?" He put the broom away. "Aimee, I told you I would do the sweeping. You should be sitting down. The doctor said the baby is going to come any day now, and you need your rest."

"Matthew, I'm not that fragile. It is only a little bit of sweeping."

Her husband sauntered toward her and braced his hands on either side of her against the wall. He kissed her softly, and Aimee lost herself to the feel of him. It was two years since their wedding day, and he still caused butterflies to dance inside her.

Matthew broke the kiss and gently caressed her belly. "I am excited to meet our little one, love. I know you are going to be a wonderful mother."

"And you are going to be such a loving father. Our baby is going to be very happy." Aimee rested her hands atop his.

He leaned in again to kiss her, but they were interrupted by a knock on their front door. Matthew sighed. "We can continue this later, princess. Please, sit down." He nudged her toward the chair in the entryway.

Another knock sounded on the door, this one more urgent. Aimee wondered who it could be, as their town was not very populated. She already knew every person who lived here, as it was mainly just a place of refuge for people who had suffered the earthquake that had hit the island several years ago. Matthew had selected this town as their place to live precisely because of how quiet it was. So far, they had not entertained a single visitor in their little house on the cliff that looked out over the bay.

Matthew glanced back at Aimee before opening the door. Aimee could not get a good view of their visitor from the chair she was sitting in, so she craned her neck around her husband.

"Mrs. Archer! What a pleasure," Matthew said. "Aimee, darling, come over here and greet our guest!"

Matthew did not have to ask her twice to come see her best friend. Aimee rose as quickly as her growing figure would allow and sped over to the door. As sure as could be, Eden was standing on the other side of the entryway. Her curly, brown hair had fallen loose from its updo, and Aimee suspected she knew the culprit. A young girl with matching brown hair sat against her mother's hip and tugged at Eden's hair. Eden's towheaded stepson, Reed, stood at her side, much taller than the last time Aimee had seen him.

Eden tugged Aimee into an embrace. "Oh, it is good to see you, dear. Letters help me stop worrying about you, but they do not stop me missing you!" The little girl in Eden's arms reached out toward Aimee.

Eden chuckled. "Usually, Clara is afraid of anyone but Caspian and me, but she does love Uncle Gage and now it seems as if she loves Aunt Aimee already."

"Can I hold her?" Aimee beamed. The sight of a happy, healthy baby made her all the more excited for her own.

"Of course!" Eden handed the girl to Aimee, and the little one began chewing on Aimee's hair.

Matthew patted young Reed on the back. "Do come in." He held the door for them. "Where, pray tell, is your husband and your other little one, Mrs. Archer?"

Eden smiled as she followed Aimee into the house. "Caspian is on his way. He got delayed with Cedric. He was stopping to show him every little thing, but Clara and I were excited to see you."

Aimee could not wait to meet her friend's other child, Clara's twin brother. She hugged Clara close and lowered herself into the chair. It was a little cumbersome to carry her with her swollen belly.

"Aunt Aimee, isn't my sister adorable? I love her so much." Reed rushed to her side, brushing a lock of Clara's short hair out of her eyes.

"Yes, Reed, she is adorable."

"Reed, are you bothering Mrs. Emery?" Caspian's booming voice startled them all.

"I don't think I am, Papa. Am I bothering you, Aunt Aimee?"

"No, not one bit. Hello, Captain Archer."

Caspian offered her a quick bow. The baby boy he held squirmed in his arms and reached for his sister. Caspian distracted Cedric by tossing him in the air and catching him.

"Were you all starting the festivities without us?" Ivy also appeared and sped into the room, carrying her newborn baby boy, Brodie. Gage was directly behind his family, the man's customary grin on his face as he held their adopted daughter, Emma. Addie, Gage's sister, and Adam, Eden's brother were close behind. Adam's arm was around Addie, and her cheeks were bright pink. Aimee noticed the new engagement ring that adorned her finger.

Ivy went straight to Aimee's side and hugged her.

"Welcome to our little home, everyone. I am afraid we were not expecting visitors this afternoon. To what do we owe the pleasure of seeing all of our friends?"

"We were not certain when we would be blessed with the presence of Aimee's little one, but we all wanted to be together again. It has been too long since we have seen each other, and what better excuse to get together than a new baby?" Ivy cuddled her baby boy closer against her chest as she spoke. Eden edged closer, fawning over the little one.

"Well, now I feel quite pressured, don't I?" Aimee laughed, rubbing her belly. "The doctor said I am due any day now. I appreciate the effort everyone made to visit us!"

"I am sorry to say we do not have the room to accommodate everyone in our little home." Matthew stroked his wife's shoulders as he spoke.

"Oh, not to worry. We have made accommodations down in town," Caspian offered. "We thought you would need your space with your new baby, so we planned accordingly."

"Thank you for your consideration." Aimee glanced around the room, filled with more true friends and small children than she had ever seen back home in London. However, that phrase was old to her now, for London was no longer home to her. Home was right here where she had been tossed together with her husband and her new child, surrounded by her closest friends. And she was happy. They all were.

The End

About the Author

Bestselling author Heather Manning is a young lady who loves to read—and write. Her first trilogy, Ladies of the Caribbean, quickly became bestsellers. After graduating from Stephens College with a degree in Theatre Arts, she moved to Orlando, Florida where she works in the hospitality industry. In her spare time, she enjoys kayaking, hiking, and biking through all of Florida's beautiful State Parks.

You can connect with me on:
- https://www.heathermanningofficial.com
- https://www.facebook.com/heathermauthor
- https://www.instagram.com/heatherm_author

Subscribe to my newsletter:
- https://mailchi.mp/e5e9e7498f8e/join-my-newsletter

Also by Heather Manning

Dancing through history with a hint of adventure.

Swept to Sea, Book One, Ladies of the Caribbean

Lady Eden Trenton never wanted to leave her privileged existence in London—until her father invites a dangerous suitor into her life. Left with few options, Eden devises the best reprieve she can: escape. Chasing freedom, she stows away aboard a pirate ship, praying she will gain her independence in the colonies before she is discovered by the nefarious crew.

Captain Caspian Archer has spent the last five years hardening his heart and searching to exact revenge for the event that tore his life to shreds. When he catches word that his enemy is residing in Jamaica, Caspian steers his ship toward the colonies in all haste. His plans soon change, however, when he discovers the young beauty hiding in his ship's hold.

Cut from the only lives they have known, Caspian and Eden are pulled together as each pursues a fresh hope upon the sea.

Carried Home, Book Two, Ladies of the Caribbean

The Caribbean is no place for a society lady of London, yet after a daring quest to save a friend, Lady Ivy Shaw finds herself trapped far from home. Now, driven with worry for her young brother, she is determined to return to England in all haste. So, when a new acquaintance offers to sail her to her brother's side, she jumps at the offer, scarcely caring that the man is a privateer.

Captain Gage Thompson is just learning how to be a captain. He sailed for years under the command of his longtime friend, Caspian Archer, but serving a captain and being a captain are, as he soon discovers, two very different roles. While struggling to gain the respect of his newfound crew, he now faces the distraction of beautiful Lady Shaw. He finds himself entranced by her and promises to give her passage home.

After a brief stop in Port Royal, Ivy and Gage discover an abandoned child. They both decide to bring her with them on their voyage to England. But problems soon arise in the form of hurricanes and enemy pirates, and Ivy and Gage find themselves scrambling to not only care for a lonely child, but also gain command of a motley crew.

Will love bud between Ivy and Gage as they journey home?

Stuck in Time

Ember Appleton thought she was in for a lousy afternoon when she got stood up on a blind date—little did she know she would end up in the wrong century! Focused on her love of art, Ember pays little attention to the world around her, until a freak accident sends her whirling back into Kansas City, in the year 1933. There she witnesses one of the city's most gruesome catastrophes in history right before her eyes. However, her day gets a little brighter when she is rescued by a handsome, concerned reporter who cannot take his eyes off of her...

Daire Kelley has worked his whole life for this moment–an opportunity to capture history the moment it occurs and cement his name as a world-class reporter. That is until a bewildering woman materializes in front of him, stopping him in his tracks and catapulting him into a quandary he never expected: capture the crime of the decade on camera or rescue the intriguing woman who is standing in the crosshairs of the biggest mobster shootout in Kansas City history.

Danger lurks in every corner of 1933 Kansas City, a city run by the powerful mafia machine. Can Ember survive the unexpected dangers of this complicated era? And will Daire be forced to set aside his lifelong dreams in order to keep them both alive? These two may be stuck in time, but could they have found each other for a reason?